The

Aurora Bear

A.C. Winfield

The Aurora Bear

ISBN-13: 978-1981209101
ISBN-10: 1981209107

For Rowan x

Acknowledgements

Oh my goodness there are so many of you to thank over these past few years! From my friends, family, to my betas, to those who follow my page on facebook, twitter etc. Also to Ben for all your love and encouragement. But I think the most important thank you of all goes out to all of you who read my stories.

I must point out this book is dedicated to a young lady called Rowan. She tells me with huge enthusiasm that she reads my books over and over again. This is for you Rowan. If it wasn't for you and many other boys and girls who shown me encouragement over the past couple of years of writing this story, The Aurora Bear, book 4 to Ebony's Legacy would most likely still be tucked away on my laptop and not see the light of day. Hold on tight as the adventure is only just beginning!

Ax.

The Aurora Bear

CHAPTER 1
GOLDEN

*A*s I stirred, my head felt very heavy.

I opened my eyes. In front of me was all but bright, golden, wispy vapours. I reached out. My hand twisting and turning. I twiddled my fingers as I watched the strange mist dance. As I stood up and watched, it swirled around me in a great, big vortex. I reached forwards to grab hold of the vapour strands, but it simply fizzed away. My heart grew sad. I felt alone. None of the vapours touched me. It was as though, like the light before in the Underverse, the golden mist was afraid of me.

Afraid. I realised now that I could not see, hear or even feel any of the pack around me.

I jumped up and down, trying to see further with hope of finding someone but there was nothing. Nothing but golden mist which rolled on and on into the far distance. "Raff?" I called, my voice echoed around me. A tear rolled down my cheek. I watched the golden coloured mist again, it reminded me of the golden hound. "Nubis?" I hiccupped. I missed her.

Suddenly there she was. The smallest of all the Night Hounds with her shaggy, golden fur. "Nubis!" I cried with delight. I ran forwards, and without any hesitation, I wrapped my arms around her broad, furry shoulders. I was so happy to find the Night Hound here in this strange, empty, echoing place. Her Soul Song so loud in my ears, my fears simply fizzled away.

She nuzzled me, bowing her head, pulling me in tightly with her chin. Her chest rumbled with content. "Hello dear little one." I frowned as I looked up at her. The Night Hound seemed different somehow...

My head tilted sideways as she looked down at me. The same light that lit the Underverse throughout our journey here rippled through her fur, making it look like she was in a constant breeze...

Wind!

Suddenly there was a lot of pain. My head no longer feeling fuzzy but too full of...

Something. I scrunched up my fuzzy, black hair with my fingers and I closed my eyes as I cried out in pain. In an instant a flash of colour burst in front of my eyes. Material, flapping in the salty-smelling spray. It made my nose sting. I remembered...

Another flash and more pain. Red, blue, yellow and black. A picture of a bird flapping against a bright blue background. Sky! Again, pain shot across my forehead followed by a warmth tickling my goose bumped skin and then, nothing but a spot of coolness. I felt the coolness pressing onto my forehead.

Soothing the pain away. As I opened my eyes slowly, blinking at the fuzzy light, there she was. The strange hound with the golden, rippling fur. The cold spot, I came to realise was where Nubis was pressing her leathery, wet nose against me. The golden hound stepped back.

4

"Nubis, what's going on? Where are we? Where's the pack?" I knew I asked way too many questions, way too quickly for her to answer them all but I couldn't help it.

Sitting on her hunches, with her golden fur glowing brighter than ever before, Nubis' eyes gleamed happily. Changing their colours from warm brown, a deep sea blue and a cold, stony grey. These were all familiar to me…

I shook my head. I couldn't remember why.

She chuckled. "So many questions little one. I thought you only had one?"

"Who am I?" I replied. Unable to stop myself. I gasped, covering my mouth wondering where the question had come from. Nubis lowered her head until she looked at me right in the eye. Her eyes dimmed until they were all but black as the Underverse's sky. For the first time since I can remember, I grew afraid of her until I shook on the spot. Her Soul Song grew louder and louder till my ears rang. I clutched at them. The song was strange. Full of power I did not understand. My eyes grew large and round.

The hound blew the golden mist into my face. This tickled my skin slightly, whispering in my ears and clouding my mind with their thick, wispy tendrils.

"Remember, Ebony Night." Nubis's voice echoed through the swirling, golden mist. "Remember those who are forever in your heart or be lost forever." With those final words the golden hound's fur grew brighter and brighter. Everything turned blinding white as Nubis the Night Hound with the lonesome song shimmered and then vanished into thin air.

Chapter 2

First Memory

*G*randfather and I loved walking along the little cove. Now I have my best friend Hale, the Comet Cat, it's even more fun.

On the other side of Ladon Manor's gates, over the other side of the North Road, hidden slightly by the bushes and small trees was a gateway leading down to a beach by the estuary. I loved this part of the

Manor's grounds. It was like our own little rocky paradise. You entered by going through an iron gate. Though it was never locked, passers-by never seemed to see it. I was only allowed to go there when my Grandfather, Sunny, or Marsha or even 'Strict Bea' was with me because it was over the Manor's boundary wall but I loved my time there all the same.

Hale and I loved to collect all the shells we could find. Filling the bag until it was bursting at the seams. Then we would lay them out in pretty patterns. These patterns made with shells always reminded me of Bob Macy's little hut garden. It was full of multi-coloured pebbles. Some blue, some red, some purple and some green. They were arranged in such a way they looked like flowers and hedgerows. I liked to arrange my patterns so the lines on the shells connected with the others making star burst patterns. They reminded me of fireworks exploding in the night sky.

One day, I noticed something other than shells or colourful pebbles on our beach. There was a piece of netting and caught up inside the wired squares was a bird. Hale and I ran over to it to try and help but the bird had already passed over Ladon's scaly back into heaven. It wasn't a very pleasant sight. Hale leapt up in my arms and I wiped a tear away with my free, sandy hand. "We were too late." I told Hale and he bumped his velvety nose on mine. Comforting me.

Grandfather walked over to see what we had found. He bent his creaking knees, picked up the netting and the bird gently in his bony hand, shaking his head.

"Why did the bird get caught up in the net, Grandfather?" I asked, hiccupping.

"Sadly Ebony, people do not care or think what they are doing to Ia when they leave their rubbish behind. Each item we leave behind must go somewhere and sadly in this case it has caused this bird to drown."

"They did this on purpose?" I asked, amazed. My brown eyes grew wide.

"Sometimes, sometimes not. They do not think about the consequences. Such as this netting," he said, gently putting the bird back down on the sand. "Or that rope," grandfather said pointing to a bundle of blue and white rope tide up in a mess. "Or even that can," and he pointed to an empty tin can half buried in the sand. Mine and Hale's mouths dropped open in a very large 'O'.

"But how can they? Ia is such a wonderful place. Why spoil it with all this rubbish?" I watched Grandfather shrug and he groaned as he stood up.

"I do not know, Ebony. For once, I haven't got the answers."

"There must be something we can do?" I told my Grandfather and Hale, the little Comet Cat now sitting in my arms. I looked at the dead bird again, my heart sad. I looked at the bag Grandfather was holding, ready and waiting for the shells to be placed inside. Then I had an idea. I placed Hale gently back on the ground.

Both my Grandfather and Hale the little Comet Cat watched me as I carefully took out the bird from the netting and dug a little hole for him. After placing the bird inside and burying it back over with sand, I gathered up the netting and placed it inside Grandfather's bag.

"What are you up to, Ebony?" He asked, peering into the bag we used for collecting shells.

"I'm tidying up." I told my Grandfather. I ran over

10

with the bundle of ropes and placed them inside the bag too. Getting the idea, Hale the Comet Cat carefully unburied the tin can with his clawed paws and Grandfather helped by picking it up and placing it inside the bag along with the bundle of rope and the squared wire netting.

"Just because some people don't care about Ia," I told Grandfather running back with another piece of rubbish, "doesn't mean we don't." I could hear Hale running behind me and turning I saw him dragging a deflated buoy, the sort fishermen used to cushion their boats as they brazed alongside the harbour's wall. Grandfather and I smiled at one another before running off and helping Hale who was struggling with its sodden weight and placed the buoy inside the bag as well.

After another hour, we had scoured every nook and cranny of the little cove, from one end to the other. Clearing up each discarded item. The bag was so full, we had to carry a few items.

"What are we going to do with all this?" I asked Grandfather.

"I'll think of something," he replied. Grandfather's

grey eyes flashed mysteriously. Hale and I grinned.

From then on, once a week, Hale, Grandfather and I would clean up the Ladon Manor's little cove. By the time we had finished, the rocky beach would sparkle and shine in the star light. Sometimes, when we were running late, Mother's star, the Northern Star, would shine brightly down upon us. Pinpointing objects our eyes did not see down here on Ia...

Suddenly the scene in front of me fizzled and faded from view. Its' colours running into one another until another memory took its place...

Today, today was my birthday. To start off with Hale, Grandfather and I, even Sunny and his wife Marsha, had a naughty breakfast of cake and jelly. Grandfather announced "Well it is your birthday after all, how many times does anyone turn ten?"

Both Hale and I yelled "Once!" making everyone laugh.

While Sunny and Marsha stayed at the manor that evening, Grandfather took Hale and I down to the little cove. The waves crashed into one another like bashing symbols in an orchestra. The salt water jumped up high into the air like Jack Rabbits. The waves were crowned with bright, white foamy crests. Both Hale and I ran towards the most inviting midnight sea blue. I closed my eyes and took a deep intake of salty air. I loved it here. It was wonderful!

I felt a nudge and looking down I found it was Hale, nudging me with his foot. "Ebony, what's that?" I opened my eyes and looked to where he was pointing. Not too far away, in between the lapping sea and frothy sand, something gleamed. Hale and I looked at one another and then at the same time, raced towards it. Maybe it was buried treasure? A chest full of gold coins? The treasured items flashed in my mind, one after the other and I imagined what me and the Comet Cat were about to find. We came to a sudden halt for there in front of us wasn't a treasure chest full of gold coins but something that turned out to be something so much more special.

My bare feet sunk into the wet sand as the surf splashed and swirled around my naked toes. I frowned. From the top of my head down to the bottom of my nose my skin rippled. I picked up the object. I crouched down so Hale could have a closer look, turning it over in my hand.

"What is it?" I asked in a whisper. I didn't understand. It looked just like an ordinary pebble but somehow I knew that it was something else... something more.

"I don't know." Hale replied. His voice just as low. "Let's go and show your Grandfather." We ran back to Grandfather who was watching us closely from not too far away.

"Grandfather!" I cried. I saw Grandfather's silhouette wave.

"Hellloooo." He called back. We both didn't stop until we had reached him. I bent over, hands on my knees trying to get my breath back. "Woa! What's all this about?" He asked grinning ear to ear. I held out the pebble.

"We. Found. This." I told grandfather, breathing heavily. Running across the sand was hard work.

"Did you now. Hmmm…" Grandfather took the pebble shaped like a heart from my open hand. As he twilled the heart-shaped pebble around I saw its colours sparkle and shine. The pebble was black as the night and glistened all blue, purple and white in the light. Hale and I watched my Grandfather with wide eyes. "You know what this is, don't you?" He asked me and we shook our heads. "This pebble is a Sea Heart. A gift from the sea to you, Ebony." And Grandfather placed the pebble most carefully back into my hand and closed my fingers around it. "Many people of Ia have forgotten Ia is a living, breathing being just like you and me. I think it's the sea saying thank you for all your and Hale's hard work." Grandfather smiled at me kindly, winking.

I knelt down so Hale could have another look. I did not know if Grandfather was teasing me but the pebble was certainly something special. The little Comet Cat, with his large diamond green eyes, stared at the Sea Heart and both at the same time we breathed: "Wow!"

As the sun sunk below the waves, turning the sky to all shades of oranges and pinks, Hale the little black Comet Cat shimmered into his twin-tailed Comet Cat form as the night creeped in. Grandfather called us over. He was sat inside one of the old lime kilns. There were three along this beach, nestled in amongst the trees. They hadn't been used for a long, long time but I loved them all the same. They made ideal shelters to set up camp fires to tell my stories. But today was my birthday and Grandfather decided it was his turn to be the story teller.

"On windy days, the sea was thrown into such frenzy, the white crested waves formed into White Horses." He began "The White Horses would wake up from their slumber. They would gallop and skip

16

across the wave's surface. Their manes fanned out behind them." I turned my head quickly, expecting to see one but sadly there weren't any White Horses that rose up from their slumber to gallop and skip across the ocean's surface this night. Maybe they will appear later?

I turned back around and saw my grandfather smiling at me. His grey eyes twinkling in the dim star lit night…

I will always remember that. My heart sank. How could I ever forget grandfather and my best friend Hale?

Suddenly Raff's face swirled in front of me. His grey eyes, I realised, matched my Grandfather's in each and every way. I felt my heart thumping, the force of which rippled out into the golden mist now foaming in front of me as the scene around me dimmed. As the wispy fingers touched me, I had a very bad feeling about the next memory. Did I not want to remember more? I felt something on my cheek and touching it. I realised I was crying. But why?

Once again the golden mist and its light vanished

from sight until I was back on the beach...

Hale and I started drawing the outline of a White Horse on the beach. My Grandfather watched on as we sculpted the Sea Horse rising out of the sandy ground.

The Comet Cat helped me collect starfish for the

horse's constellation just like my mother's Star Bear's fur. We collected flat, multi-coloured pebbles for its hooves and seaweed for its mane. The sand glittered brightly in the dim star light. This Sea Horse was really as beautiful as my mother, brave as my father and as clever as my Grandfather. This Sea Horse would be just like them, I told myself.

When we finished, we sat by the fire, melting marshmallows with Grandfather. Hale and I were laughing, seeing how many marshmallows we could pop into our mouths before chewing. Hale was Ladon Manor's record holder!

"Your father wanted you to have this," Grandfather told me as he gave me a domed-shaped, metal box. It had a little flap at one end and when I looked through it I could see little pin holes. Little eyes looking up at the starry night sky. As I looked more closely, little etchings joined up some of the pinholes like a dot to dot game.

"If you line these up with the stars above," he told me, "it will tell you the star's names and the constellations that they make." I hugged my Grandfather and he smiled back at me.

"Will father come visit us tonight Grandfather?" I asked, knowing the answer already. He was a captain of a pirate steam ship and a protector of Ia's sea after all. Grandfather stroke a stray bit of frizzy, black hair behind my ear.

"I am afraid not, love. He wanted to. So much. So does your mother," I saw Grandfather look back behind me. Turning I could see my mother's starlight battling through the clouds but even the stars didn't have the powers over the nature of Ia's elements.

"It's ok." I told them both. "I understand." And with that, my mother's star dimmed slightly. Not giving up the fight but relieved I forgave them both for not being here tonight. I felt Grandfather kiss me gently on the head.

My father's gift was amazing but my mother's was the most beautiful!

Grandfather presented me with a gift wrapped in a bluest, silkiest of silks. "I found this on the door step last night," he told me, placing it in my hands. As I unwrapped my gift with shaking hands, shimmering star dust fell onto the sandy ground. Inside lay a wooden heart that fitted perfectly in the palms of my hands.

My mother's gift was created from a beautiful mixture of little bits and pieces of drift wood that were all white, yellow and blue. The bits and pieces of wood were smooth to the touch, their little lumps and bumps fitted perfectly together, slotting into place like a jigsaw puzzle. On my beautiful wooden heart shaped gift were shells and feathers just like Grandfather, Hale and I used to collect. They shimmered in the star light. Something each from the land, sea and sky but my favourite part about my Mother's gift was in the middle of the wooden, drift wood heart.

In the middle was a heart-shaped hole and when I pulled out my pebble, which was black as the night and glistened all blue, purple and white in the star light from my pocket, it fitted inside the heart-shaped hole perfectly!

I clapped my hands together, full of excitement making Hale and Grandfather beam with delight.

"It's a dream catcher," Hale told me, now looking at it closely. "It'll bring you good dreams and fend off the bad ones." I nodded and hugged the heart tighter to my own.

"Thank you, Mother." I called over the crashing waves as I ran towards them, waving up to the hidden star. Her hazy light twinkled back behind the clouds, the wind blew softly. I closed my eyes, imagining it was my mother's hand, brushing my hair away from my face gently.

"Happy birthday, my little Ebony." She seemed to

whisper ever so softly in my ear.

Chapter 3
Choices

"*N*O!" I yelled, finding myself in the field of golden mist once again.

"Ebony." I twirled around, half expecting my mother in her star-studded dress standing before me. I sobbed when I saw it was only Nubis. Half out of relief, and half in heartbreak. "Ebony." Nubis's voice was so soft and gentle making me breathe more easily.

She came forward and brushed her golden-furred cheek along my own, wiping the salty tears away. "I know it's hard. It's hard on all who must pass through the mists of memories but you must remember if you are to choose to return to your family." The golden hound told me.

"Return?" I hiccuped. The Night Hound stepped back and gave me a toothy grin, her furry chest reverberated with a soft hum. Nothing like a normal dog at all. I remember now. The Night Hounds reminded me of mother when she was in her Star

Bear form. She too hummed me a lullaby once, after saying goodbye to Abigail, making me go to sleep as she carried me on her back, back home.

For the first time since arriving in the Underverse, I felt a warmth. The golden mist of memory covering me like a soft warm blanket. I liked this memory. I remembered Father, Captain Blake of the steam ship Fire Crow holding me tightly in his arms. He was warm. The smell of the salty sea on his clothing.

Suddenly my nose stung from the memory of the salty smell. Soothing away my fears for a short while...

"Who are you, Nubis?" The giant hound tilted her golden head to one side. Her one, deep sea blue eye on me. Her one ear perked and the other flopped down. For a giant hound she looked kind of cute. She looked at me for a while. Her eyes turning back to the ever changing tones. Grey like my grandfather's and Raff's. Deep sea blue like my father's and then brown, flecked with gold just like mine and my mother's. Half-curious, half-sad.

"I am Nubis, daughter and loyal servant of the Star Dog, Canis Major." As she spoke, a memory came flooding back to me. A giant three-headed dog who was the guardian of the gateway to the Milky Way. My heart beat fast. Faces seemed to rush passed me, swirling and forming magically in the golden mist. My mother running in her Star Bear form. Father standing on board his steam ship as it puffed and billowed over the crashing waves. Grandfather spinning me around in his bony arms. Hale the twinned tail Comet Cat rubbing against my leg. Ghosts of all those I longed for. I tried to touch each and every one but they all puffed in a wisp of golden smoke before I could get close enough. No Hale, no Grandfather. No Mother, Father or even Bob Macy. What was happening? I didn't understand. The thoughts echoed in my mind. I did not know where I was! Suddenly my chest felt very tight, I couldn't breathe!

"You have not lost them, Ebony. Not yet." Nubis sounded like her father, the Star Dog, Canis Major. Full of power and authority. "You and all the Night Hounds have fallen into the Underverse by no fault of your own."

"The Night Hounds? They're still here then, they

haven't left me?" I asked in relief. Nubis nodded, her eyes changing to a glowing emerald green. Hale's!

"Yes, the Night Hounds are here. My father, Canis Major, transformed them many years ago giving them their Night Hound bodies. Their memories erased as they crossed into this sacred realm. They were all sent to the Underverse involuntarily by the Eternals who wish to destroy the balance of our kingdoms." My eyes grew wide at hearing the Eternals name. "But," Nubis growled now, her chest reverberating, "you do not belong in this realm Ebony Night, your fate lays elsewhere. My father did not transform you into a Night Hound. He's trying to help you. It is up to you to remember who you truly are. I am sorry to say the memories you have remembered so far were the happier memories. You have more to come if you wish to continue your journey back up to the land of Ia."

"Up?" I asked, frowning so my forehead wrinkled in a funny way from the top of my head, all the way down to the tip of my nose.

Nubis bowed her head slightly. "The Underverse is an ancient kingdom, where everything began. Even the stars above began in the Underverse." My mouth dropped with a soft pop. Nubis gave her funny kind of laughter again and I couldn't help but to smile. Her tail wagged twice before stopping. I had a feeling that's as much wagging that the Night Hound, Nubis, ever did. "You had the word from my father, you have the support of the stars. But he cannot come in person for this land is forbidden by all who dwell in the sky so he sent me instead. Being a creature of the land of the living and of the dead, I can travel where I am needed." I swayed on my feet, Nubis's words slowly sinking in.

"I am... Dead?" The words made me feel numb from the top of my head to the tip of my toes.

"Not quite," Nubis replied. "Your soul has been separated from your body in a very unnatural manner. A forbidden way. Though there is still time for you to regain your memories, you need to hurry, for your soul will fade completely here without some sort of body." She nodded her golden furred head towards me and as I raised my hand, I was amazed to see it was see-through, almost matching the mist surrounding me perfectly. "The Night Hound, the one you named Raff, has a similar choice to make. Remember what makes you you, Ebony Night, daughter of Stella Maris, the Northern Star and daughter of Captain Blake of the steam ship Fire Crow. Both blood and souls of the stars above Ia. However painful it is to remember, live once again. Your family, friends and Ia need you more than you ever know. The more you remember, the more whole your soul will become and your path home will become clear. Forget, then you will simply fade away."

I thought about my best friend Hale, the Comet Cat with his twined tails who only appeared at night. Grandfather with his cheeky smile and mischievous eyes. Mother in her magical Star Bear form. Her star shining brightly on a clear night sky, guiding my father, on board his steam ship, The Fire Crow with his mighty pirate crew. Once again they formed before me. Running, sailing, waving in the golden mist. My heart felt whole. I looked up at Nubis and she at me. Our brown, golden streaked eyes matching one another in each and every way, just like Mothers' and I.

As I thought about my friends and family, I watched opened mouthed as my hands became more and more solid until I was a ghost no more.

"Thank you." I said, curtseying.

"You are very welcome Ebony Night. May your light shine bright even on the darkest of nights." And with that, the giant golden dog bowed her shaggy head as her form shimmered away as though she was never there…

Chapter 4

Reunion

*A*s the golden mist fizzled away, a bright light shone down upon me. I had to screen my eyes to see. As my eyes adjusted I saw I was surrounded by high walls. I couldn't move, my feet were glued to the spot, my body turning cold as the stone around me. The walls felt like they were staring. A hundred pairs of angry eyes looking down at me. Just like Nubis and her father, Canis Major the Dog Star, they hummed with powers I did not understand. I was so small and they were giants. Nubis told me this was where everything, even the constellations, began. Was this the star's birth place? Was that the power I could feel now?

A howl rose up to what seemed to be all around me.

Something moved. The golden mist clung to a shadow galloping towards me. Another howl. An angry howl as something thrashed inside the golden vapours. My heart was beating ever so fast. "Raff?" I

32

called over to where I saw the shadow. Hoping, wishing it was Raff the Night Hound. The shadow came closer and closer until it blacked out the white light filtering through the dancing golden mist.

"Raff?" I pleaded. My voice shaking. My ears drummed to the rhythm of my very quick heartbeat. I could not hear Raff's Soul Song. Was it him? Was it Nubis or was it something else coming to hurt me?

The mist swirled around the shadow's mouth, where it breathed in and out heavily. Suddenly the shadowed creature fell out of the golden mist as though it was pushed from within.

I screamed. I tried to pull away but something furry had pinned me to the floor.

Its voice was first a hum in the back ground, its face still a blur from behind the tears that had found their way to the surface as I fought my way out of the monster's grip. I tried once again to pull away with all my might. Kicking, screaming. "Ebony, it's me! I won't hurt you." I stopped. Froze.

As I turned, the pressure lifted and there in front of me was a familiar yet, not so familiar face. His eyes looked kind but also very worried. "Hello Ebony

Night." Said the voice and I couldn't help but to smile.

"RAFF!" I yelled, giving him the biggest bear hug I could muster and he nuzzled me back. Hugging me with his big, strong paw. He held me so tight air rushed out of my lungs but I didn't care. As Raff held me, deep within I could now hear the familiar Soul Song of the Night Hound. It hummed with content.

Pack, pack, pack! He sang.

Pack, pack, pack! Mine sang in return.

"Raff!" I cried. I was so happy to see him.

"Hey you." Raff said, as he eventually let me go. He wiped away my tears that had escaped with his black, leathery nose and ruffled my hair with one of his hairy front paws. I giggled as I ducked out of his reach.

"It's so good to see you, little Alpha." He told me and I nodded. I was relieved to have a friend by my side.

"Raff?" I asked.

"Hmmm?" He replied. His eyes scanning every part of me. From my frizzy hair down to my bare, now whole, yet still pale toes. I wiggled them.

"Where's the rest of the pack?" I asked, looking around us.

Raff kept his eyes on me. His expression I did not understand. I remembered Father when we first met. As though reading my thoughts, a few of the golden wisps returned, transforming into my father sitting on his captain's chair with all sorts of pulleys and leavers just like when he told me that I looked just like my mother and had my father's hair. "Turns out it's just me." Raff replied, watching the form of my father, Captain of the steam ship Fire Crow fizzle away. "Gift of Canis Major and all that."

"You met him too?" I asked, my mouth falling wide open to a very large 'O'. Raff was grinning widely. I did not know why but I suddenly remembered my grandfather running around as he chased me shouting 'TAG!' Grandfather would always cheat when it was my turn to chase him. He would find the highest branch, in the highest tree, waggling his tongue at me calling "Na, na, na, na, naaa!" As he took out the most sugary, sweetest sweet Bea had hidden earlier but Grandfather always had a knack of stiffing them out. Bea would tell him off afterwards for eating them all and for ruining his best suits as they would always snag in the trees. But Grandfather didn't care about his clothing. Grandfather and I found the game funny.

It took a lot of effort not to laugh as the scene playing out in front of me in the small amount of mist now lingering around us.

"No, but I heard you did." Raff replied, sounding strange like he had a frog in his throat. I nodded but I wasn't looking at Raff. My mouth went up on one side as I struggled to not laugh at the memory of Grandfather still playing tag in front of me. Raff nudged me gently with his giant black leathery nose bringing me back down to Ia with its coolness. I nodded. "Nubis told me I needed to help you with your last memory." He told me. My mouth hanging open again, so wide Grandfather would have told me I would catch flies.

"You'll catch flies." Raff said, tapping my chin gently with his soft paw. I frowned. "And if the wind changes, you'll stay like that." Raff said winking at me.

"That's what Grandfather would have said."

"Ebony Night," Raff asked gently, I felt his grey eyes boring into mine. I looked into his. He blinked and as they did so the greyness became softer. "Ebony." He sighed, his voice sounding unlike the Alpha I once knew. Instead it sounded kind, gentle and protective like Grandfather's. "You must think. Nubis said you had the key of finding the way out. Your gift from Canis Major himself. Do you know what she means?" I shook my head and then, stopped. "Are you sure? Ebony please think. This is important."

Just then another memory came back to me…

*

It was getting late. I could no longer hide my yawns and rubbing of my eyes any longer. I got up from the fire. Standing beside the Sea Horse, Hale and I had made earlier that night, I looked down at the sand sculpture which glistened in the hazy moonlight. With its star fish constellation, pebbled hooves and seaweed mane. I frowned, something was missing…

The Sea Horse was as beautiful as my mother, brave as my father and his eyes made him as clever as Grandfather but someone was missing…Then it came

37

to me. Me!

Suddenly the stars seemed to have awoken. The sky became clear and the stars danced way up high above, twinkling in their black, blue and purple starry heaven high in the night sky. The brightest of them all was the Northern Star, my mother. She winked at me and I smiled back.

The sea was ever so loud tonight. I visualised it leaping for joy. Crashing together, like symbols in an orchestra. The waves jumped high like jack rabbits, sending sprays of salt water into the air. I imagined the Sea Horse to be beautiful as my mother, brave as my father, clever as my grandfather but he still needed something else...

I looked down at my mother's gift, the heart she gave me made from the land, sea and sky. Taking the pebble I found earlier that was as black as the night, glittering all shades of blue, purple and white in the star light. As I took it back out of the dream catcher's hole, I placed it on the Sea Horse's chest instead. I looked up at Mother's star which twinkled merrily against the dark night sky.

"There," I said looking back down at the sand sculpture in front of me. "now the Sea Horse is as beautiful as my mother, strong as my father, clever as my grandfather and has a heart gifted from the sea, given back by me." I turned to the others watching me.

"His name is Murdock." As I announced the Sea Horse's name, I felt strange. My ears popped like a storm was brewing. I felt tingly all over from my head all the way down to my bare sandy toes.

As quick as a flash the sky burst to life. Neon green waves rippled from the horizon up and over our heads…like the lights in the Underverse!

I flung my arms open wide and laughed as I spun around in a circle for a better view. The sea and sky looked like they were dancing with one another. Their movements matching one another in each and every way. While waves leaped and waved, the neon colours jumped and swayed. The echoing dance was mesmerising.

"The aurora borealis," Hale the Comet Cat breathed. I could see his ears and tails twitching in the eerie green light. "I have heard of it but never thought in all my nine lives I would get a chance to see it."

Just then the sand started to shift, tugging at my sandy, bare feet. Slowly at first so it tickled them gently, making me giggle and then faster and faster it raced across the surface. As though it was being sucked backwards. All three of us watched on motionless as the Sea Horse stood up!

Mine and Hale's mouth dropped with a pop!

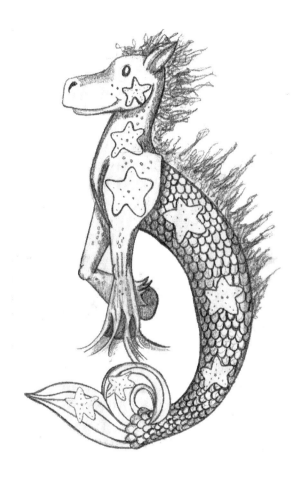

"Neiigghhh!" Murdock said as he swished his mane to and fro, gouging the wet sand with his stony hooves. "Oh, wow!" I breathed. As the Sea Horse swished its mane, particles of sand went soaring through the night air. The sand trickled up the horse's legs, soon renewing those that he lost.

The Sea Horses' black shiny pebbled eyes were looking straight at me!

At first I couldn't move but then it winked. I smiled, taking a step forward. This Sea Horse wasn't dangerous, he only wanted to be friends.

"Ebony no!" A large hand clamped over my stomach, dragging me down. Just as we hit the sandy ground the Sea Horse reared up, neighing loudly. Sand falling, pelting down on us from Murdock as he leapt over us, sailing high through the air. My head snapped to the side, my eyes glued to the now galloping creature as it ran along the sand until SPLOSH! The Horse landed into the surf before raising above the white crested waves. Neighing contently, he swished his sopping wet green, seaweed mane side to side and just like that, skipped off merrily into the night. His neigh echoing into the night.

"Murdock, come back." I called quietly to the now dark sky, reaching out, hand clenching onto nothing but salty air as I wished for the Sea Horse to come back to me. It was too late, Murdock the Sea Horse was gone.

"Ebony? Ebony!" It was Grandfather calling my name. My eyes pulled away from the waves where Murdock vanished from sight. As I turned, I watched as Grandfather scanned my sandy face. "Did that creature hurt you?" It took a while for me to understand who he was on about. I shook my head really fast.

"Murdock wouldn't have hurt anyone, Grandfather" I told him as he helped me up and dusted the wet sand off me. Grandfather sighed and I had a strange feeling he didn't believe me…

"Do you think he'll ever come back, Grandfather?" I asked. But he didn't seem to hear. Both the Comet Cat and I were watching Grandfather now. His eyes were all scrunched up, the lines on his face even deeper than before. He looked really old! Was Grandfather worried about Murdock? I know I was. Would he ever come back? Would he be safe? Would he find friends out there in the wide, deep, blue ocean? "Grandfather?" I asked again. Tugging at his tweed coat gently to get his attention. Hale meowed gently, leaping into my arms and I caught him like I always did.

Slowly, Grandfather's head turned, looking everywhere but at me. His crinkled face normally warm and gentle, as I have always remembered him. Now however, his eyes seemed alert and afraid as he scanned the bay around us...

Hale meowed again softly. He wasn't looking at me or Grandfather but out over towards the sand banks where the mouth of the two rivers met the sea. "Someone is watching," he said so quietly.

"Ebony, let's go. Now!" Grandfather's voice was nothing like I ever heard before. And ever so quickly, he slung everything back into the picnic basket. I quickly scooped up Father's gift and Hale carried Mother's carefully in his mouth. As quick as a flash Grandfather snatched my hand and off we went, back to the Manor just as the stars said good morning to the ever encroaching daybreak. Before Grandfather closed the heavy front door with a mighty bang and slid the heavy bolts across, I managed one last wave to Mother, who twinkled desperately down at me.

"Ebony..." She seemed to whisper my name on the

cold breeze.

White light blinded me and then another memory hit me with full force…

One week had passed since Hale and I were forbidden to leave the confines of the Manor. Grandfather didn't give us any explanation apart from: "It's for your own good." Since then Bea had been sticking to us like really sticky glue. "Surely Grandfather wouldn't ground me forever?" I asked Hale, who followed me downstairs to breakfast.

The hallway was dark. All the curtains and shutters were closed, blocking out the sunlight outside. We were forbidden to open them ever since that night we made Murdock.

Wafting up the stairs, along the winding corridors until it met our nostrils was the most wonderful smell. Hale meowed, uncertain. I sighed and followed it.

Both mine and the Comet Cat's stomach growled. We looked at one another. My brown, golden-flecked eyes meeting his blazing green. Without a word, we quickened our step.

As we reached the dining room, where the wonderful smells smelt the strongest, our bellies started to rumble even more. As we entered the room occupied mainly by the very large, oblong table we found everyone sat around it, including 'Strict Bea'. Marsha whipped me up scrambled eggs and tomatoes on toast - my favourite - while Hale had a bowl of warm milk. The little black Comet Cat with his speckled belly lapped at his bowl, his little pink tongue slurping the warm liquid at a super-fast speed. His bright green, diamond eyes grew bigger and bigger with every mouthful. Today he had his favourite bow tie on. Sometimes Marsha, Hale and I would have a dress up day. Marsha and I would spend many hours sewing, making Hale all sorts of tiny waistcoats, some midnight blue in colour, some with a tartan pattern, some that sparkled like his belly at night and some even matched Grandfather's to a T! Grandfather would walk in, wondering what the raucous was all about, making us all fall about laughing. I think Hale took his role of the Cat of The Manor very seriously.

Since living here, Hale had been looked after well by my Grandfather, Sunny, Marsha and he was even a favourite with 'Strict Bea'. She loved picking him up, stroking his fur and tickling him under his chin. She even smiled every time she saw him. I thought 'Strict Bea' should smile more often, it made her look young and pretty. Hale was shy, he didn't talk much around everyone else but that was ok. My friends and Grandfather seemed to know what he meant by his little mews and blinking of his bright, green diamond eyes. He was adored by all, even when his form fizzled and changed in front of their eyes. They weren't frightened by his Comet-Catness. Hale's head would grow slightly too large for his body, his speckled furry chest glittering with star light and not to forget his other tail reappearing for another night. Grandfather loved the transformation, he would give Hale applause and ask for an encore, but of course, we would have to wait for another night until we could witness the marvellous transformation once again.

"Your grandfather is running late," Hale mewed quietly to me, nudging me gently with his soft velvety nose. Marsha pushed another portion of egg onto my plate before I could get a chance to ask for more. She knew me far too well. "Has he got a client?" I shrugged, fork still in my mouth.

"I don't know," I mumbled around it.

"What was that?" Marsha asked, looking between me and Hale kindly. I was surprised she didn't tell me off for talking with my mouth full.

I pulled the fork out of my mouth with a soft pop and swallowed. "Hale was wondering where Grandfather was?" I answered her question, as I looked at Grandfather's empty chair positioned at the head of the long table. As I looked around I watched Sunny and 'Strict Bea' opposite us as they ate their own breakfast. Sunny, already on his forth portion scoffed his own scrambled eggs at a fast pace with a "Yomp, yomp, yomp." Me and the little black Comet

Cat looked at one another, my mouth twitched while his green diamond eyes glittered amusingly. It didn't matter how many times I saw Sunny eat like that, I still found it funny. With my new found best friend it was even funnier. When Hale first joined us at the dining table for the very first time, I had to nudge him with my bony elbow many times to stop him from laughing.

"I don't know…" Marsha replied, soothing her boy, Ozzy who wiggled and giggled in her free arm. Her brow frowning slightly as she thought long and hard. I noticed she was wearing one of the dresses I loved so much. It was made of a velvety, emerald green material, with lace trimming on the sleeve and neck. Sometimes Marsha would give in to me asking over and over again, would get it out of her wardrobe and let me try it on. Though it was much too big on me, it was still fun to dress up. "I don't remember him saying he had a client this morning…"

"I'll go and check on him." Sunny said as he polished off his plate, leaping to his feet. "Knowing your grandfather, he is probably buried underneath paperwork and forgotten he has to eat."

Another flash of blinding bright, white light.

Though it wasn't the sunniest of days the rain, wind and lightning stayed far out to sea so Hale and I played in the shelter of the lake and woods. We sailed wax coated paper boats, our cheeks puffing out, my face growing redder and redder as we blew as hard as we could until the boats were in the middle of the lake and no longer in reach. We fed the red squirrels. Hale found it the hardest to convince the red bushy-tailed critters to come down and feed from his hand but with time, the squirrels began to realise this little, black cat with his strange bow tie, speckled belly and diamond green eyes wouldn't harm even a fly…well maybe a fly but definitely not a squirrel.

Just as the third squirrel came out of hiding, Hale's ears started to twitch. The squirrels nattered to one another making their red bushy tails flick in alarm. Suddenly they darted, one even scampered over my shoulder and up the pine tree, clambering to the branches way up high.

"Bea's calling for you. She sounds worried." The little Comet Cat informed me. His ears now swivelling back and forth.

"Shhhh!" I said, putting my finger to my lips and hushing him with the flapping of my hand.

"But she says to come inside if we have snuck outside." Hale whispered back but I gestured again. I knew 'Strict Bea' couldn't hear us from here but I didn't want to go inside and have lessons today. Today was a time for adventure.

We stayed low and quiet for some time until Hale said: "She's gone." We breathed again. Hiding like this reminded me of the times I hid in the library when either 'Strict Bea', Grandfather, Marsha or Sunny came looking for me. It gave me an idea.

"I have seen that look way too many times," Hale told me. I felt my face turn a bright shade of rosy red. Hale laugh softly. "It's ok," he reassured me. "I haven't been on an adventure for aaaggggeeessss. Whatever it is, I'm in!"

*

I knocked. We waited but no reply. I knocked again, waited and still no reply. I placed my hand on the door knob, looking at Hale questioningly. He blinked. I turned the handle, slowly and with a click, the door swung open. "Grandfather?" I called but no reply. The candles around the room were low. He had clearly been here. "Wonder where he could be?"

"Maybe he's gone for something to eat…" I looked over to the entrance way leading to mine and Hale's most favourite room in the whole of Ia, the library, with its painted ceiling where two star bears circled one another. Tonight though the double doors were closed. Unlike the library this room was plain in colour. White with golden dado rails around the outside of the room, complete with matching candle holders, floral patterns tumbling down the wall from where they stuck out. The most magical item in the highly polished, stark white room which gave you a clue of the treasures in the room next door, was the bedroom's four-poster bed. Heavy oak carved with Ladon, the dragon constellation winding his way up the giant four bed posts while Ursa Major and Ursa Minor on the matching oak head rest watching over the slumbering occupancies. Just like me, Grandfather loved my mother's art work. They were the only splashes of colour that broke up the pure white, high walls but this room was no longer used as a bedroom. This was my grandfather's study.

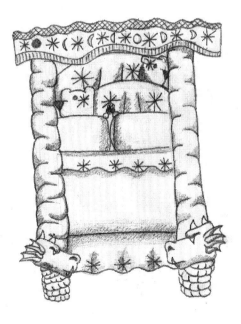

Grandfather told me once this used to be my mother's room. Maybe that was why he liked to work in here, to be closer to mother…

But this room was dark now. Like all the shutters and curtains in the whole of the Manor, they too had not escaped this strict rule. They had to stay closed.

In the middle of each of the very tall shutters, a beam of stark white light shone through. Warming the room.

Near to the middle floor to ceiling window was Grandfather's desk. It was red in colour and looked odd in this room somehow, like it shouldn't be there. The only way it matched the room was Ladon, the mighty star dragon, carved into its surface. His clawed feet and legs held up the table, his shoulders and back the frame from which the desk's surface sat upon. His gem-like eyes bore into my own, like he was alive. They glittered angrily in the flickering candle light.

Once again I looked over at the closed double doors that led to the library.

"I'm in if you are," I said. Hale didn't reply but together we approached the double doors slowly, one foot in front of the other.

My hand clenched on the handles, quivering with excitement. "On the count of three" My voice was all but a whisper. I looked down into the Comet's Cat's diamond, green eyes. They blinked at me. "Three!" The stark white, double doors swung open to reveal the most spectacular room in the whole of Ladon Manor, the library. Shelf after shelf. Books ranging from the size of Hale's paws up to the size of myself made the wooden platforms groan under so much weight. And there, painted above was Ursa Major and Ursa Minor encircled by Ladon, the magnificent dragon constellation.

Though I had been here thousands of times before and Hale, many hundreds since living here, it didn't stop us taking a deep breath.

"Wow!" We breathed in unison.

*

"Don't worry," I told the twin tailed Comet Cat as he and I lay on our backs staring up at the painted ceiling. "My grandfather always told me," I deepened my voice, mimicking Grandfather "When something seems to disappear, it'll appear when it wants to be found." The two of us laughed, for my impersonation of Grandfather was rather good. Since Hale and I arrived, we had searched high and low for the little book with its crinkled cover with most of its pages falling out. But as hard as we tried, I nor the Comet Cat, who was still wearing his fetching bow tie, could not find the book anywhere.

"Why don't we come here anymore?" Hale hissed, careful to keep his voice down. I was pleased to see the library hadn't changed since the last time we came here. The painted ceiling with is two encircling Star Bears and Ladon the mighty Star Dragon was alive as ever!

I remembered Grandfather telling me this was also his daughter's, my mother's, Stella Maris - a Star Bear in human form - most favourite room in the whole of Ladon Manor too, and I could understand why.

"Ebony?" Hale asked, making me shake myself slightly from my daydream.

"Because I am too big to fit into the secret hiding place." Hale looked over at the window seat where we usually hid. When Hale came to live here, I showed him all my favourite places around the Manor, including all my hidey holes.

"Yeah," he said "it was a bit of a squeeze last time." Hale and I laughed. We were laughing so much at the memory of the both of us being tightly packed into the tiny little window seat in the magical painted ceiling library, we had to hold our hands over our mouths to muffle the sound. We didn't want to be discovered.

When we eventually stopped, Hale told me "everyone grows, Ebony. You are just becoming a lady. How old are you now?"

"Ten," I told my best friend, the little Comet Cat, Hale and, with his whiskery head, nodded.

"See. In normal cat terms that would be really old and your fur would be all grey." I giggled. "Maybe you will soon be big enough to sail the seas with your father and play along the tightropes in the night sky with your mother."

"Do you really think so?" I sat up excitedly and then covered my mouth once again, for I had been a tad too loud. Hale and I strained our ears, listening hard to the make sure it was the old Manor that was creaking and groaning and not because someone, namely my grandfather, was making his way across the floor boards back to his study.

"Clear." Hale announced and we both breathed a sigh of relief.

"I know so." Hale eventually replied to my question, nodding his whiskery head at me as we both rolled back over to face one another. Now laying on our bellies, on the soft comfy rug under the painted night sky. "Your father doesn't take you to sea for you are too small and young for a human and therefore it would be way too dangerous to have his daughter on board his ship. Now that you are getting older, you are both smarter and stronger." Hale's fangs gleamed in the candle light as he grinned at me while I grinned back at the Comet Cat with his twitching black, fluffy tail.

"Imagine me a real life pirate, living on the high seas!" I whispered excitedly.

"And me, a steam ship's cat. I would be chasing rats all day long!" Hale licked his chops.

Hale and I stayed a little longer in the library dreaming of living on my father's pirate steam ship, the Fire Crow. Sailing the seas, tackling sea creatures that lurked beneath the waves and finding hidden treasure on deserted islands. "A pirate's life is surely for me." I sighed.

"And for me." Hale whispered back excitedly.

*

Time was getting on. With still no sign of Grandfather, both of us thought it was best to go before we were caught. Hale led the way with his tail held high in the air. I decided to have one last look at my grandfather's study before saying goodbye. That was when something caught my eye.

Sitting on Grandfather's desk was a box. This box was unlike any other I had ever seen before. "Strange." I said as I found myself stepping back in through the doorway.

"Ebony!" The Comet Cat hissed. "If we wait any longer, your grandfather will surely find us. It won't be long until the sun goes down, I can feel it, my whiskers are twitching. We should go!"

"In a moment." I whispered back, unable to take my brown, golden-flecked eyes off the strange little box. I stepped up to it, inspecting the box more closely.

The box was circular in shape and silver in colour. Its surface reflecting the gold in the narrow beam of sunlight. What intrigued me the most was its shape, for it was most unusual. The little round, silvery box was in the shape of a tree stump and on four of its corners, silver roots seemed to have grown downwards. The roots curled underneath itself. I picked up this strange little silvery box and turned it over. The roots continued underneath, entwining in a never-ending loop.

"Ebony, we should go." Hissed Hale again. When I didn't reply he bounded back into my Grandfather's study. "What are you doing?"

I placed the little circular silvery box with its tree stump-like appearance and roots entwined in a never-ending loop down on my Grandfather's desk once again. Watching it in awe.

I could feel the Comet Cat watching me closely. In the corner of my eye, his tail was twitching. But I didn't turn, my eyes were only for the box, like it had put me under some kind of spell. "Come and look at this." I beckoned him from across the room. Hale seemed wary of the strange box but he crept ever so slowly, closer and closer to my side.

"What is it?" he asked, his fur raised on end. Hale sniffed the air. "Star dust!" His voice all but a whisper.

"I don't know." I replied slowly. Picking up the strange little circular, silvery box with its tree stump roots entwined in a never-ending loop once again. My fingers found their way over its lid, feeling for the box's latch.

"Ebony don't!" Hale meowed at me loudly but it was too late. With a loud click, I had opened the box. Hale panicked and leapt onto the desk, trying to knock the box from my hands but his rescue attempt didn't go to plan. Instead of landing smoothly in front of me to swipe the box away, he landed on some of Grandfather's papers and they and the little black Comet Cat went skidding to the other side of the desk. Grandfather's papers went flying everywhere!

I watched in horror as Hale tried to grab hold of something, anything! Including the desk lamp but it was no good. The lamp too went crashing to the ground. The Comet Cat managed to turn over just in time. As he toppled over the edge of the desk, Hale reached out one last time, claws fully extended to their longest and sharpest points. Hale was holding on by a claw!

"Hale," I said, reaching over with one arm as I

helped him back onto the desk. "You are a silly cat,"

"But there's stars at work here." Hale informed me as he jumped, managing to find a paper-free spot this time, on Grandfather's desk. My mouth popped opened. "It's too late now, you've opened it. What's inside?" He asked unable to stop himself.

As he placed his furry paws on the edge of the circular, silvery box I was holding, the black cat pulled it down slightly so he could have a closer look. Inside a kind of golden mist swirled. As it eventually evaporated away, inside laying on a deep blue silk-cushioned lining was a key!

Hale and I drew a sharp intake of breath, for the key inside matched the box perfectly. The key looked to be of the same silvery-type of metal, bark like pattern of knots. Lines marked along its sides as though the key was grown rather than made. The looped handle on top was covered with silver branches and along these branches were leaves but they weren't silver like the rest of the key. The leaves were made of finely cut crystal, echoing the colours of the turning season for this time of year. With deep browns, burnt oranges and bright canary yellows.

"It's a Tree Key!" The Comet Cat and I said together. We looked up from the key to each other and beamed.

Suddenly there was a shout from down the corridor. "Ebony?" Our faces matched each other as we both looked up at one another. "Ebony? Is that you making that racket?"

"Grandfather! Oh boy," I swallowed.

"We're in trouble." Hale finished my sentence just as the Lord of Ladon Manor came striding through his study's doorway.

"Ebony Night, what are you doing in my study?" I saw my Grandfather's eyes grow wide as he took in the mess around us. Scattered sheets everywhere, claw marks marked deeply into his desk's highly polished surface. And a broken lamp now shattered on the floor. "Good grief what a mess!"

"I'll clear it up." I turned around quickly, trying to pick up the papers and other scattered items, trying to tidy the mess that both of us had made only a minute before.

"No," he said. I paused, swallowed again. For Grandfather sounded very annoyed. "I need you and Hale to pack a bag," He told me. I frowned. Did Grandfather wish for us to leave Ladon Manor forever because we made a mess?

Grandfather shook his balding head, smiling a strange smile. He didn't look happy, his eyes were too watery for that, so why did he smile?

"Me, you and Hale" He started to explain "are going to go away for a little while." My and Hale's jaw dropped. I had never left Ladon Manor in all my life.

"But why are we…?" Grandfather raised his hand, silently asking me to ask no more questions. I swallowed. For a moment, Grandfather turned around and when he turned back, his eyes looked slightly red. I frowned. Grandfather looked a little upset but that strange small smile was still on his face.

"Think of it like a vacation," he added. "You've been cooped up in this Manor for far too long, everyone needs a holiday sometime. See new sights and all that. It'll be good for us all. Oh and Ebony,

64

Hale," we both blinked up at him in silence, unsure what to say or how to react to the news of us going away. "I do not want to hear you have been in this room again without my permission…When we come back, alright?" Hale and I both nodded.

"Sorry Grandfather. We will be good." I promised.

"Sorry, Lord Ladon. We promise we will be good." Hale apologised, and at the same time both me and the Comet Cat crossed our hearts.

Grandfather chuckled. Both Hale and I looked up at him in surprise, making the old man laugh even more. Tears now visible, glistening on his bony cheeks. "You are so much like your mother." He told me. "No one could ever mistake you for not being so." He paused, scratching his grey beard agitatedly. "Well then?" He asked "What are you waiting for? Go and get ready. An adventure awaits. Go, go, go!" Grandfather clapped his hands and ushered the two of us out of his study's door, still with that strange small smile on his face.

The memory fizzled. Colours merging together. The last of all to merge was my Grandfather's face. I was staring at him. Trying to work out what his face was trying to tell me.

Chapter 5
The Tree Key

"*E*bony? Ebony?" I heard Raff's voice like it was far away. "Ebony!" he yelled again and I felt myself being shaken.

"Raff?" I asked. Still in a daze.

"Oh thank the stars. Are you alright?" he asked, taking his giant clawed paw off me and kneeling down to my level, looking me in the eyes. Feeling my forehead like Bea did when I was feeling unwell. "What happened?" Raff asked. His voice full of sadness and concern.

"Another memory…" I replied and with some hesitation, I stuck my hand in my pocket. I felt what I was looking for. I breathed. I pulled it out and showed Raff. "Me and my friend Hale, a Comet Cat. We called it a Tree Key." Raff smiled at me. I didn't know what he found so funny.

"Tree Key, Comet Cats…you do have a strange life indeed, little cub. Well then..." Raff said, standing up and looking around him. As I did the same, I realised there was a window shimmering in the shadows of the high wall. "I think we may have found our ticket out of here."

*

The Tree Key was in my hand, shaking in its keyhole, waiting to be turned. The window was made out of grey stone, the same colour as Raff's eyes, shaped like a small arch way. Inside that one was another, then another and so on until the arches were so small it fitted around the Tree Key, creating a tiny keyhole. I guessed there were other windows around me but the dark shadow hugging the curved wall would not allow me to see and find out for sure. Though I didn't know why, I knew deep down within they weren't my windows and so were forbidden to enter.

My hand continued to shake, clanking the tiny metal key against the cold stone. The shrill ringing hurt my ears but still I couldn't stop shaking. This window felt like it was a secret that shouldn't be unleashed. If I listened hard enough I could hear voices coming from within, beckoning me to come to them. They were so enchanting, so welcoming, it frightened me. "I don't like it." My voice was shaking as much as my tightly clasped hand.

"I know you don't Ebony but this is the only way to reach those who are waiting for us on the other side. You miss your Mum and Dad?" Raff the Night Hound asked and I nodded. "How about that Comet Cat you told me all about? Hale?" I nodded again, wiping my nose with my free hand. My heart ached from not having them here beside me. I longed to see them again. "I'm right here beside you every step of the way alright?" I felt a gentle nudge on my shoulder as Raff brushed his head along it, like Hale sometimes did when he was letting me know he was there. I looked back. Raff was right beside me just like he said. His soft grey eyes, reminding me of my Grandfather's, reassuring me. I nodded. Without looking and before I could change my mind I turned the Tree Key in its grey, stone hole with a very loud CLICK!

Instantly there was a blinding light. I threw my hands up, shielding my eyes. Then, as quickly as it appeared, the light vanished and in its place was a deep, dark hole. For the first time since finding myself here in the Underverse there was a breeze. A faint sort of whistling coming from the opening where the arched window had opened. Impossible dew covered impossible cobwebs framing the stone's outer rim.

The outside world seemed one step away…

But still there was that feeling again. Like something bad was waiting for me on the other side. The whispering voices ahead of me. There was nowhere to run. To escape.

I looked back and Raff gave me a reassuring nod. "I'm right behind you." Nodding in return, I turned to face the deep, dark hole with the impossible breeze and impossible dewy cobwebs.

"Here goes." I gulped. As I took a step forward, the moment my toe nudged just over the edge of the stony sill, it felt as though giant hands grab hold of me. I screamed. I was thrown forwards. I hit the stone walls over and over again. Tumbling down a never ending deep, dark pit. I was knocked here and there. I tried to grab hold of something, anything, but the walls were too round and smooth. I wasn't sure which way was up nor which way was down. In the darkness, in the ever-falling, the only comfort I had was Raff's voice, calling my name over and over again but the air was sucked from my lungs making it impossible for me to reply. I felt my brain go fuzzy, like a thick, thunderous cloud blocking out the sun, turning the sky black as the tunnel. Then, when I thought I could not think, see or feel any more, darkness swallowed me up and I fell into blissful sleep.

Chapter 6

Torn

I felt my collar being pulled as I was lifted off the ground and then back onto my unsteady bare feet. I blinked the sleepiness away. "Ebony, are you alright?" My eyes grew wider as I looked around. Raff sat beside me, looking down at me with his big, grey eyes. They were full of concern but my attention was drawn away by something else…

Or rather someone else. Even though it was dark, there was still a little bit of light shining through. I realised then it was Mother's star. My heart pounded. We were back on Ia! She seemed to be trying to fight her way through the dark, thunderous clouds swarming above our heads, banging on the door of the thick, cloudy sky. Her light grew bright and then dimmer once again. Was she trying to tell me something?

"What is that? Lightning?" Raff asked. His big hairy forehead winkling underneath all the worry lines.

"Mother." I whispered in reply. I felt like there was something in my throat. Like I had swallowed something too big. She wasn't far away but I knew she could only come down on clear nights.

I heard Raff whisper a name. Did he just say "Stella", my Mother's name? Before I could ask him, there was movement ahead. Raff grabbed my coat's sleeve with his sharp teeth, carefully pulling me behind a big pine tree.

Looking around I realised that we were home! There was Ladon Manor, just like I remembered it. We were on the drive way, behind was where the trees bowed themselves over. 'The Squirrel Highway' both me and my best friend Hale the Comet Cat called it because this was where the squirrels loved to jump from one tree to the other. Here, they didn't need to worry about coming down to the ground where foxes and other woodland creatures could catch them to have them for their supper.

I was smiling at the memory of the trees when I heard my Grandfather's voice. "Ebony, we must hurry." He said in a tone I have never liked. I jumped for there in front of me was…

Me! Like someone was playing a scene out in front of us and Raff and I were the standing audience.

Did the doorway allow both me and Raff into another one of my memories?

I saw one arm of my double had Hale the little black Comet Cat tucked underneath it while the other had a bag full to the brim with my clothes and other items that I could never dream of leaving behind.

Hale was shimmering slightly, his extra tail twitching side to side. He mewed sadly, looking up beyond the tree's canopy. Did he sense the urgent calling from my mother like I did now? But past-Ebony's eyes were only for our home, Ladon Manor.

I grew very sad. I now knew the answer was yes, this was a memory playing out in front of us.

"But, when will we be coming back?" I heard myself asking.

"I don't know." Grandfather replied. His voice was full of sadness. It was strange. I knew what they were about to say and do but only a moment before.

I saw my past self's mouth drop open in a very large O. "What?" she asked. Her expression and tone full of surprise and fear.

"I will tell you all that you need to know when we have got far enough away. Now come along quickly!" Grandfather paused and then added a soft, "Please." Grandfather pleaded, taking past-Ebony's elbow but I watched as my past-self came to a complete halt.

"We're leaving…for good?" She asked.

"I don't know." Her grandfather replied. He was so distressed I didn't recognise his voice now. It was so unlike Grandfather to be so angry…so upset.

"No." My past self's voice was so quiet, I had to strain my ears to hear her from where me and Raff stood behind the big pine tree.

"Ebony?"

"No!" I jumped once again. Now my voice taking me by surprise. Past-Ebony had tore her arm away from her Grandfather before snatching Ladon Manor's key from his slacked hand. I heard a tear ripping through the air and as I looked down at my own coat's sleeve, there I found a wide, gaping hole. My heart sank. It was true. These events really did happen...I swallowed.

Dropping her bag, the past Ebony ran back to the Manor. Slamming the huge wooden front door behind her with a mighty BOOM!

"Ebony?" I heard Raff call out to me. I had stepped out from behind the tree and started walking towards Grandfather.

"They won't be able to see or hear us, Raff." I said, unsure how I knew but it felt right. I felt his warm grey eyes on me now. As I looked back I saw his eyes were full of empathy. The hairy worry lines were deeper more than before along his furry head. His once powerful grey eyes now looking much, much sadder. Matching my grandfather's eyes as he looked up at his daughter's star before running after past-Ebony.

I walked, not ran, up the gravel path. I didn't need to keep checking behind me. I could hear Raff's soft paws just behind me crunching on the cool, gravel drive. I reached behind and he came to my side without hesitation. He sat while I stood. Raff lent into me gently, reassuring me he was still there for as long I needed him.

Grandfather banged on the door trying to convince my past self or Hale to allow him to enter. We watched him try every single ground level door and window, rattling them furiously but they were all bolted. He had made sure of that himself. The Manor was on lock down even before leaving.

I sighed and the scene froze.

"I don't want to see any more." I said, shaking my fuzzy, dark haired head so much the long, dark, fuzzy waves covered my face like curtains. Raff hummed. His whole body vibrating next to mine.

"I know it's hard, Ebony," he began as I buried my face into his furry brown-grey coat. That bad feeling grew stronger in my heart. "But you can do this." Raff the Night Hound continued to tell me. "I have seen how strong you are when you commanded me not to attack Nubis. Whatever you have to face, we will do this together. As a pack… as a family." My breath got caught in my throat and I hiccupped. I nodded, Raff's furry mass pressing comfortingly on my side. I rubbed my face, took a few more deep breaths and just like that, it was like someone had pressed play again.

Goose bumps rose on my ghostly arms. Grandfather was shivering too and above me, my mother's starlight beat its fists on the stormy, dark sky but still they both did not give up on me. My grandfather's voice was getting hoarse, shouting up to my balcony window, trying his hardest to beckon me outside. Then, Raff stood quickly and started to growl in the direction of the trees. It took me a few moments until I saw what his sharp eyes and ears picked out from the almost-black shadows. From the shadows cast by Ladon Manor's mighty trees, figures appeared. All hooded apart from one. A lady.

She had burnt amber hair that billowed around her narrow face like red hot flames and her eyes were like Hale's. The deepest green but they were not kind like my friend, the Comet Cat. They were fierce and wild!

"Hello Rufus." She said my Grandfather's name like she was greeting an old friend. I breathed a sigh of relief. Maybe this was a friend of his after all? But then the flickering starlight caught Grandfather's face. The storm above reflecting in his steely, unfriendly, grey eyes. I have only seen that look a few times. Whoever this lady was, she was no friend of his.

"Hello, Amber Jade," he greeted her coldly.

"Nice place you got here," she said, looking

around, admiring the Manor in front of her. Her men laughed, their deep booms disrupting the chattering night calls of the waders down below in the water meadow.

At this point the wind began to pick up. The trees bowing and buffering against its howl. Like a prowling cat creeping closer and closer to its prey. It was as though nature itself had sensed something bad was about to happen. "I have always wanted to see it for myself you know. After hearing so much about it, blah, blah, blah." She told Grandfather, twirling her hand around in a funny way.

"Really?" Grandfather asked, not sounding like he believed her at all.

I could see movement as my past self who was now silhouetted against the panes of glass in her bedroom's balcony doors tried to see who the other voices belonged to.

"And that must be…" the lady, Amber Jade began to say, following his gaze. "Ah yes, little Ebony. Seriously Rufus. You thought you could hide her away forever? How cruel you lot really are." She pouted, wobbling her lip before giggling a high-pitched laugh.

Her laughter made my very head tingle as my hairs stood up on end. A cold shiver made its way down my spine. I didn't like this Amber Jade. She didn't seem nice at all.

Suddenly I heard a smack and then a very loud crunch. Both my past-self and I screamed. Covering our mouths in shock and surprise as Grandfather fought with one of the large hooded men. There was very loud smash. The front door's window pane tinkled as the multi-coloured picture of Ladon the Star Dragon tumbled down, broken into unfixable pieces. These pieces glittering for a few moments in the beating star light until the twinkling died, as the last piece tumbled to the floor. If I wasn't so shocked by the fight, I might have been saddened by the broken picture. This was one of my favourite things about Ladon Manor after the library's painted ceiling.

Watching on, I realised the giant man had tried to get in and Grandfather was fighting him back. As though a distant memory had fluttered down and settled itself on my shoulder I knew what was about to happen. I wanted run, to hide, to…defend!

"Grandfather!" I yelled but I had forgotten Raff. He scooped me up around my middle, holding me back easily with one gigantic paw. "Let me go! Grandfather! Please Raff, I must help him."

"Ebony he can't hear you. We are both on a different plane to them. That's why I think we can't interact with the others around us. We are like ghosts to them. You can't help him..." Raff's voice faded away as Grandfather stumbled away from the giant, hooded man. It was too late. I had waited too long. If only...

Grandfather's hand was clenching his side. His back was to me. As he turned, his eyes unbelievably transfixed onto my brown golden flecked eyes. "Ebony, you are so much like your mother..." He breathed with half a smile. His last words, his last smile before collapsing on the gravel floor. My heart now shattered like the window pane.

"Grandfather!" Both my past-self and I screamed again. Raff let me go. I fell forwards and crawled to my Grandfather's side. I found him still breathing. Still blinking. "Grandfather." I breathed unsteadily, unsure he could hear or see me. I tried to pull the dagger out but my hands simply passed right through it. I wasn't really here I reminded myself. All this had already passed. I was already too late.

"Well, that was easy." Amber Jade told her men, rubbering her hands together and their laughter boomed around us, drumming against my ear drum painfully. Amber Jade walked up to my dying Grandfather "You are one lucky old man," she told him, kneeling down on the opposite side to me. "I was going to let you suffer but never mind. I will just have to settle for your granddaughter instead." Hot, steaming, salty tears were tumbling down my ghostly cheeks. Looking down at Grandfather, I saw his warm grey eyes transfixed on my own. His mouth moving, speaking my name over and over again silently. His hand clenching air as he tried to hold on to me.

"Being at Canis Major's door must allow him to see and hear you, Ebony." Raff told me gently. The Night Hound sounded like he had swallowed something too big for him. "Say your goodbye whilst you still can."

"But I don't want to." I told Raff angrily in torrents of tears. A strange smell, a metallic tang brushed away the salty spray and luscious grass I knew so well that belonged to the nights of Ladon Manor, my home. Everything felt like it was being torn away from me.

"You must." Raff replied stiffly and after a moment, nudged me gently with his cold, leathery nose before stepping away to give me space.

I tried to stroke my grandfather's face, his arms too weak to reach me now. But I could not touch him. My ghostly form, not of this world, just passed through. Unable to find the words, his grey eyes softening as they took me in. I tried to speak but every time the words got somehow lost along the way. "I don't want you to go." Were the only words that managed to eventually find their way out.

One last breath. Grandfather's eyes dulled. Ghostly pale, like my skin now. He was gone. I kissed his forehead, now able to touch him. Much too late.

I didn't scream, I howled.

Chapter 7

Thundering Paws

I Found myself in a dark tunnel. Running. The thundering continued but it was all around me now. Inside I felt them, the Night Hounds. My pack was here with me. We were running together.

I howled again and so did they.

PACK! PACK! PACK! We sung in unison.

I felt a breeze. We must be close to the surface now.

Allowing the Night Hound's senses to flood my own, I ran even harder than before. The hounds heard my cry. They howled for me.

PACK! PACK! PACK! The Night Hounds sang back once again in unison.

Suddenly a shadow moved beside me and before I knew what was happening I bumped into something, or should I say someone, so hard I landed with a bump on the dusty, hard ground.

"Raff!" I called out in surprise. I blinked. One moment I could hear and feel the drum beat of the pack, their Soul Songs singing all around me but now it was as though someone had plugged my ears full of wax. It was just me and Raff. Alone.

He looked me in the eye with his midsummer storm eyes. He hummed. His whole body reverberating before me. His strength flooding through me.

He did not say anything. He didn't need too. In my heart I knew what he was trying to say to me. He was part of my pack after all. Not because I was an Alpha but because he was my friend…"Friends?" I whispered. My throat enclosed the word making me cough.

Raff snorted. It wasn't laughter like many people on Ia would have thought it was but it was a sigh of relief. His lone Soul Song told me so.

I looked around. The tunnel was now silent of the Soul Songs apart from Raff's and my own.

The other hounds ran on. Their three hundred and ninety-six padded paws thundered as they passed. I saw flashes of furs: black, white, brown, silver and even misty blue in a mesmerising blur until they completely disappeared into the small circle of light ahead. All around us grew dark and quiet.

"The Night Hound's Soul Song is so powerful, distance does not matter." Raff broke the silence after what felt like forever. The giant hound's gravelly voice echoed around us making it even more clear how alone we were. The pack was long gone.

"You called them to you in your darkest moment." Raff explained, his hot breath steaming - billowing in front of him. Looking up, only now did I realise the silver light I saw was of the rising moon finding its way through the once dark tunnel. I wrapped my arms around me. I was icy-cold. "You pulled them out of the Underverse through your grief. You, Ebony, remembered your pack when you needed them the most. Alpha or no Alpha, a Soul Song as strong as yours cannot be denied by any Night Hound. Even I felt it." Raff had his eyes closed now. His ears were flat against his head. His body shaking time to time along with mine. "Even if years pass, vast amounts of land divides them from your call. They will come if your Soul Song sings to them once again."

I leapt forwards, wrapping my arms around his

large fur covered face that was flecked with grey. I buried my face into his furry snout and as we stood in the rising moonlight, Raff begun to hum.

Raff's voice and Soul Song reverberating together until I remembered. Remembered the night I joined Raff's pack, remembered Raff soothing me to sleep with the same song. Only now I understood why it was so soothing. Grandfather used to sing it to me some nights…

For many nights after I met Mother and Father for the first time, before Hale the twined tailed Comet Cat, my best friend, came to live with me, Grandfather, Sunny and Marsha with their baby at Ladon Manor, I had dreams. I dreamt of Mother and Father. Mother running with me on her back along the cliff's edge in her Star Bear form all sparkling in the star light while father, on board his mighty pirate steam ship waved from the rocking sea below. I would wake up each and every night to find they were no longer by my side. I remembered how alone and frightened I felt in the darkness but then Grandfather would come into my room as though he knew I needed him and like magic he would sing me the song making the horrible feelings go away. The song reminded me that even though Mother and Father could not be with me, they were there. Inside my heart. Forever. Just like Grandfather was now.

More tears tumbled their way down now. I scrunched my eyes tightly, trying to stop the flow but it was no good.

I imagined my Grandfather's spirit running. Running through Canis Major's door, floating up to the Milky Way and along the mighty Star Dragon's, Ladon's, scaly back. No one knew what happened beyond Ladon's head when a soul entered Ursa Minor's realm but I hoped he would be well cared for. I hoped that Grandfather may be granted passage to the stars to be with Mother but I also knew that there must always be a balance between the stars and Ia. Maybe Mother could go and visit him instead? Making sure he had a clean suit to wear for each and every day, like he always had done back at home on Ia?

The memories of my grandfather jumping around like a giant grasshopper, his bony arms and knees creaking the way they did when he picked me up to put me on his shoulders. They were all precious memories to me. And nothing, nothing at all could make me ever forget. Not even in the Underverse because Nubis was right. Grandfather, he had a special place in my heart. Forever.

I did not know how long Raff hummed to me but I felt so much warmer, even for a ghost girl. "Hey Little Alpha." Raff said. I stepped back. His grey eyes were warm, reminding me of Grandfather's look each and every time he saw me.

"The pain won't ever go away," Raff told me. I knew he could tell the way I felt as only a Night Hound could, through our Soul Song. "But I promise it'll get easier." Raff crossed his heart just like me and my best friend Hale the Comet Cat did when we made a promise we'd never, ever break.

Raff looked back at where the pack had vanished and so did I. "They will forget us," Raff sounded very sad. "They will live out the rest of their lives, wild and free as all Night Hounds should be but they will be back if you need them."

"But what about you?" I asked, rubbing my puffy eyes. They were stinging a little. "Will you go too?" I asked. My heart gave a little squeeze. I had just lost Grandfather and I did not wish to loose Raff too but I could not tell him to stay either. He was a Night Hound. He was meant to be wild and free. I never wanted to be an Alpha again…

Suddenly I felt strange, like my body became very light.

Raff shook his head, his smile becoming even wider. He looked me in the eye for a very long time. "No, Ebony Night. My place is by your side. You and I may no longer be Alphas but our Soul Songs are the same. You are my pack, my family now."

Chapter 8

The Green Mirror

*M*y eyes took a long time to adjust to the light pooling down from the silvery orb moon. I knew we must be back on Ia because nowhere else did the night sky look so beautiful!

The Night Hound and I had found ourselves in a bowl-shaped valley. Just like in the Underverse, it pulsed with colourful light. Its steep sides full of radiant plants and sweet-smelling flowers. Behide us was a waterfall which fell from somewhere way up high. It glowed eerily green in colour in the night's light. Dotted here and there in front of us were strange humanoid statues. They were as tall and broad as Raff himself!

They stood on little rocks that sat in the shallow water as it hurried on passed. They too seemed alive, emitting a blue hue through tiny cracks. Like they were about to crack open and reveal their secrets inside. The statues must have stood there for a very long time however, because they were covered in scaly lichen and fluffy moss which swayed to its own quiet melody, pulsating, emitting their own light.

On the other side, opposite of the waterfall was a tree but it was not just like any ordinary tree. Its bark was pure white as chalk itself. It was huge, reaching way beyond the steep sides of the ferny banks. Its soft

93

pink blossomed branches seemed out of place for this time of year. They reached up so high I thought the twigged fingers could tickle the stars themselves. The tree trunk was so wide it would take more than twenty of me to wrap my arms around it. Its roots were so large and entwined with one another it created steep banks along each side of the rushing water. Arching here and there, creating intertwining wooden bridges across the rushing, cool water. The roots hugged the rocky faces and channelled the water through a tunnel. The sea must be on the other side. I could smell the salty water with every gush of air. The air so thick with grains of salt I could taste it. It was wonderful!

It was very peaceful here.

As the wisps of droplets from the cascading water danced in the air, they created multi-coloured rainbows in the moonlight. They reminded me of the Reflections on Soul Island where I travelled along the Milky Way to get Hale's tail back… It felt like a long time ago since I had been up to visit the stars.

I was about to look up, searching for my mother's star, the Northern Star, when the tree began to groan.

I frowned. It was a strange noise. As though the tree was upset about something. Its branches began to twist and turn unnaturally. Its blossom falling down around us. Despite no strong wind here the branches swayed. I frowned and Raff growled at the opening in the valley where the rushing water continued its way out to sea.

"Nubis?" I asked. I had no idea why but I just knew she was close by.

HIDE her voice seemed to whisper in my ear. The blossomed tree with its chalk white bark shook on a little breeze that blew.

Raff growled even more, lowering his body to the ground, ready to pounce on whatever or whoever was approaching. I placed my hand on Raff's furry shoulder, my fingers running through his fur.

Suddenly my head started to feel dizzy. I gripped onto Raff tightly.

"Ebony?" I heard Raff's voice ask in a strange muffled tone as though he was far away. He sounded worried.

Gripping on tighter now. My whole body was feeling strange and as I looked down, I saw I was becoming more and more see through! Like the ghost girl I was before.

My head filled with fog. I staggered along the giant tree's root and the Night Hound caught me by the scruff of my neck with his strong jaw before I could fall into the icy, rushing water below.

HIDE. I heard the voice of Nubis once more floating on the breeze. Before I could question where she was, I felt my legs dangle freely in the air. Raff had lifted me off the ground. The Night Hound turned and leapt through the waterfall! "Raff," I began, arms up, waiting for the cascade of water. I didn't get wet however, the water passed right through my see-through form. Raff on the other hand got drenched, skidding to a stop on a slippery, moss covered ledge on the other side. The valley now hidden from view.

As we did so, I felt myself slip from Raff's grip. One second I was being carried, sailing through the air with my friend, the Night Hound, and the next I strangely felt myself drift along until I hit the floor beside him. I slumped against the smooth, green rock wall just behind the roaring, falling water. "Raff, what's going on?" I asked, my head spinning some more. He looked me up and down with his warm, grey eyes. He looked really worried as he looked away. His gaze anywhere but on me. "Someone's coming," he began and then his eyes looked at the rock behind making him pause. His grey eyes grew wider and wider.

"Raff? What is it?" I asked again but he did not answer. I turned and gasped. With the rushing water behind me, there was nothing but crystal in front of me. Its surface polished to a bright sheen. Layers of different shades of greens mingled together in an intricate dance. Some areas were clear, allowing me to see even deeper into the hard rock. But it wasn't the magnificent multi layered crystal that made me stop breathing it was what was reflected in it!

In front of me was a bear. A bear just like Mother's magnificent Star Bear but also nothing alike. Its soft, thick fur was bright white, shimmering silver in the dappled light. Framing the Bear's face was a mane of midnight blue and shooting out here and there like little comets in the night sky were flecks of gold.

Matching the mane, blue and gold tipped spines

poked their way through the thick, bright white fur. Unlike Mother's bear who sparkled in star dust, a string of stars along her body. An iridescent green sheen all the way from the bottom of its nose to the tip of its very long white and mid-night blue furry tail. The colours reminded me of the arura borealis that lit the sky in a burning green on the night Murdock, the Sea Horse, came alive.

The bear reminded me of Murdock the Sea Horse. The bear was beautiful as my mother and in its eyes, I could see it was as brave as my father and as clever as my Grandfather...

I saw movement. The bear wasn't alone, there was another figure in the reflective green crystal. I thought I was going to see Raff the Night Hound, the gigantic dog-like creature with his short brown fur flecked with steely grey, matching his stormy eyes but I was wrong. Next to the bear was a man.

I looked at Raff and he looked at me and when we looked at the bear's eyes it matched mine exactly. Brown with flecks of golden here and there...

What was going on?

I opened my mouth. My body still heavy and head

still fuzzy but even before a word could come out, I heard a voice on the other side of the waterfall which made the bear's and my heart grow still. It was Amber Jade's.

Chapter 9

Capture

"*R*aff, no!" I cried but it was far too late. The giant Night Hound bounded out, through the waterfall and straight at Amber Jade.

I heard yells, growls and barks. Even with my ringing ears and fuzzy head, I could still hear him.

RAFF! RAFF! RAFF! My fast beating heart called out to his.

EBONY, EBONY, EBONY! It howled in return. PROTECT, PROTECT, PROTECT!

I ran out from my hiding place. There was Amber Jade. Once again she was not alone but this time she had even more heavily armoured men with her. I quickly counted and came to a total of twenty encircling the giant hound, and more still came, climbing up and through the tunnel of chalky-white roots.

The chalk-white, giant tree was groaning loudly. Swaying to a gust of wind that wasn't there. Its blossom falling as though they were tears tumbling their way down into the fast flowing shallow waters below. Was the tree upset?

I saw the Night Hound being surrounded by the men and I cried out loud. "Raff!" My little ghostly legs ran to him. No splashes. Not getting wet at all. My head was still spinning but I didn't care. My friend was surrounded, closed in on all sides with pointed weapons and heavily armoured men. They threw chains around him. Dragging him along the shallow watery ground. Now and again, the hound's snout would be dragged under water, making Raff cough and splutter.

"Raff!" I bellowed, running forwards, I tried to pull the chains off him but it was no good. My hands passed right through them. I was back in my ghostly form just like before! It was as though I was here but not really. But this was Ia, I knew in my heart of hearts we had returned back home. Raff could clearly be seen and heard so why couldn't I? Nubis said if I remembered everything I needed to, I could return home. I had, haven't I?

The Night Hound looked at me. His steel grey eyes growing sad. He was trapped. A Night Hound is meant to be wild and free. To run wherever his or her heart desired. Not held down in chains. "NO!" I yelled over the shouts of the men. My hands balling themselves up, my arms shaking by my side as I faced the men, ready to confront them. I wasn't going to give in…

But despite me standing right there in front of them, not one but the trapped Night Hound seemed to have seen or heard me. Instead they were looking now at Amber Jade, waiting for their Mistress's next instructions.

"Well, well, well what we got here?" I heard Amber Jade's voice echo slightly off the valley's walls. My heart grew cold at the sound of her voice. She nudged the poor, trapped Night Hound's snout under the silvery chains with her heavy booted foot. Plunging his tightly bound muzzle under water once again. Despite the lack of air, Raff growled and tried to snap his teeth at her leathery, high heeled boot. "Temper, temper. Very well, you'll make a very fine bed throw if you cannot be tamed." As she lifted her foot, allowing poor Raff to come up for air. The heavily armoured men's bellowing laughter bounced off the steep, slippery moss valley walls.

I tried the chains again and again but my ghostly hands just kept passing right through them. "Raff, I'm so sorry." Raff's soft grey eyes never left mine. He started to hum. The Night Hound hummed me the melody I knew so well now. His heart beat with my own as his Soul Song howled softly, telling me he forgave me. A ghostly droplet of salty water fell, joining the torrent of fresh as it made its way through the dark tunnel and down to the sea beyond.

Suddenly there was a mighty roar behind me. It couldn't have been the Night Hound. His snout was all tied up. Could it have been the pack coming back? But I hadn't thought of calling on them. Another roar. A roar so loud it bounced around the steep, slippery moss valley's walls making it rattle and shake. The gigantic white tree, whose roots buried themselves deeply into the river's bank, quivered!

I felt a rush of air. As something breathed down my neck. Even in ghost form my hairs stood up on end. Though the breath was roasting hot, enough to roast a turkey, I felt chills shiver through me.

I turned and there in front of me, once again, was a massive bear! Its body as big as Raff's but unlike the

103

crystal's bear, this one wasn't bright white. It was pure black as the shadow it cast along the ground around its feet. Its spines were red, hot and glowing. On the end of its tail was a deadly barb and it had wings! I could see their broken webs as they flapped helpless beneath the chains wrapped tightly around its body. But it wasn't its size, spines, wings or even the fire that licked the edges of its tightly bound, fanged jaw that surprised me most of all. Nor the fire that rolled along its spiked back. It was the bear's eyes! They too were brown with streaks of gold matching mine and my mother's in every way. But this could not have been my mother... Her Star Bear fur was not just the blackest of blacks, but the bluest of blues and all shades of mauve. Mother did not have webbed wings nor breathed fire, which danced malevolently around the bear's clamped mouth and back. Nor was it the bear I saw earlier behind the waterfall. The fire-breathing Bear stopped in front of me. I felt its gaze burning into my own. Did the Fire Bear see me?

Raff struggled against his chains, trying to get up to protect me but it was no good. The chains around him were tied very tight, held by many of the heavily armoured men ordered by Amber Jade. "Let's play around no longer." Amber Jade's voice broke my trail of thought. "Either do as I say and open the Green Mirror or I will simply use this beast instead."

Dragging my eyes away from the Fire Bear, my mouth fell open. There in amongst a guard of his own was my father, Captain Blake of the Mighty Steam Ship Fire Crow. "Father!" I cried. I heard Raff struggle even more in his bindings. The chains clinking and clanking. But the armoured men kicked him with their heavy boots, poked and prodded him with their sticks until he lay still once again. I tried to run towards my Father, Captain Blake, but as I made one step forwards, so did the strange fire breathing Fire Bear. It growled. Its eyes glowing a hue of red as it lowered its head down to my level. Yes, I thought, this bear could definitely see me.

I looked at my father, who was also bound around the wrists and ankles. He struggled with the men. He managed to headbutt one of the men who groaned, swayed and then splashed into the fast-flowing water. Seeing what he had done to one of their own, the men lifted my father and threw him into the water. Dunking his head underneath until he relaxed, and with a belly laugh the men brought him back up gasping for air.

"Not so good in fresh water, are you?" Amber Jade made her way forwards, legs sloshing through the water. Her high leather boots keeping the water out. The sneer on her face made her look terrifying! "Now what is it going to be. Your blood or the bear's?" She asked him, sneering through her teeth, pointing up to the tethered Fire Bear, trapped in the many layers of chains which clinked and clanked as the big black bear moved.

"No!" I cried, stepping once again towards my father. I was stopped once again by the big, black bear.

With a mighty pull on the chains winding around the Fire Bear's horns, it yanked the members of Amber Jade's crew off their feet, dragging them along on their belly as the Fire Bear moved, blocking my way to my father.

"What is it going to be, brother? It's an easy decision for me if you wish to test it out." She said, tapping her high healed leather boot with her very long, sharp sword.

"Brother?" I breathed but I shook my head. It didn't matter right now. Raff and my father needed my help. "Please!" I pleaded to the fire breathing Bear. "Please let me help my father." The Bear, however, did not move. It didn't even blink but the Bear continued to refuse to move out of my way. I tried stepping around once again but once again the Bear got in my way, pulling the armoured men with it.

The Fire Bear with its red fiery mane, framing its golden horns shouldn't have been able to see me but the bear could. "Who are you?" I asked the bear as it towered above me.

The men stood back up, getting their footing once again. Amber Jade's sword being held way up high. "Well brother, now is the time to make your decision or I will make it for you."

I saw my father's eyes, deepest blue of the ocean. They looked at the Bear fondly, the same look he gave me when I first came on board his pirate steam ship and he told me that HE was my father. But the Fire Bear wasn't looking at the captain now. The Bear had her hungry eyes on me. I too looked at her, looking deeply into her brown, golden flecked eyes trying to understand what she was and then I understood why the Bear looked similar to the Bear in the green crystal. Why they shared the same brown golden flecked eyes as me and my mother. Why my Father looked at this scary, giant, black, fire breathing beast in a way no one but a Father could… Nubis said my soul was separated away from my body…the Fire

Bear was me, somehow that is my body!

Before I could make sense of what I'd just discovered, my father yelled. "Mine." The captain's voice cut across me like the sharp edge of Amber Jade's sword.

"NO!" I sobbed. Raff's chains started clinking and clanking as the giant hound began to struggle and growl.

I too moved. This time however, instead of running around the big, black Fire Bear. I ran towards her and vanished.

.

Chapter 10

Fire Bear

I had no clue how I had done it but I felt my entire ghostly body merge with the Fire Bear's. We were enveloped in fire!

The Bear's instincts loud and clear: DANGER! It raged on. FIGHT! While I could only think about father and the danger he and Raff were in. SAVE THEM! I scream on the inside. The Fire Bear roared seeming to hear me.

Without a fight, the bear took over. Our heart beat fast. Mine was panic for my friend and my father while the bear's was pure rage. The Fire Bear's eyes narrowed, homing in on the lady's face framed in flaming red hair. Her green eyes widened as she watched the chains in the armoured men's hands, ping and snap from fire covered, furry body. Our internal heat intensified, radiating all over our furry, scaly body. It was too much for the metal links, now useless against the fiery ferocity.

YES! I celebrated inside. Feeling a tiny bit of hope my plan would work. WE'RE FREE TO HELP... But before I could even think 'THEM' suddenly, I was brought back down to Ia with a very loud thump.

Looking up to the top of the green hued waterfall with its cascading water snaking past the strange giant, cracked statues covered in scaly lichen and furry moss. I gulped. I could not see Mother's star in the night sky!

My human half hiccupped. The fear gripping both of our hearts, if she was able to capture my father, Protector of Ia's seas. What was she capable of doing to my mother? Stella Maris, a Star Bear in human form?

The very strong feeling of hopelessness ripped its way through me. The bear gave one almighty roar before leaping. Our webbed wings spreading. The membranes catching, snapping in the little breeze there was as my Bear's gigantic paws pounded forwards. The Fire Bear scooped up the lady who claimed herself to be my aunty. Away from her cruel men. The Fire Bear and I sailed over the rushing torrents of shallow water, over the many, many stone statues. Brushed through the cascade of falling water and with an almighty CRASH the bear's paws slammed the red haired lady into the green crystal. Amber Jade went slack in our paws. The Fire Bear, roared with delight while my ghost-self shook with fear. Our wings raised in a funny sort of umbrella as we stood on our hind legs. The roar made my aunt's hair rush back, sticking to the damp, green glass-like marble. The noise that tore from our lips told her of the pain she had caused, the torrent of emotions coursing through our veins as her heart beat on. Her head was slack, she wasn't listening! How could she not listen to how much pain we were in!

We roared again. We felt something. A tugging. The Bear self now annoyed. Like a fly buzzing around our head, we batted whatever it was, away.

I heard a yelp.

Taking no notice, the bear roared again. The Bear's black, furry and scally back arched. I could feel fire licked its way up our throat. My ghostly eyes wanted to be closed while the bear's refused, focusing on the one thing it hated most. The furnace steaming away any tears that escaped their way to the surface. I shook my head. The Bear was strong, she wanted to take over and I, in a way, wanted it too.

As the Fire Bear began to take over, another soul broke through. Desperate, my Bear slammed the unconscious body we held in our gigantic paw once more against the green, mirrored crystal. The Fire Bear's eyes twitched. I knew what it was listening to, her heart. It was still beating. Pounding. Fighting to stay in the living world, here on Ia. The Bear roared, more annoyed than anything. I felt myself start to sink lower and lower into the Bear's dark depths of consciousness. Its body, mind and soul enticing me closer and closer to the edge of no return.

'It's easy.' It seemed to whisper to me. 'No more pain. No more losing those you love the most...'

The Bear slammed her body again and again. The Green Mirror splintered, a few sharp shards bounced off our wings and body for it was protected by its scaly armour.

A howl.

A heartfelt, soulful Soul Song. Its notes settled on me like a warm, fuzzy blanket. Before only darkness but now there was light. Not red and burning like the Fire Bear's but warm, comforting, full of love...

Recognisable.

Raff!

As I thought of his name, the light grew brighter in the back of my mind.

"Ebony?" I heard him say as though from far away. I shook my head and so did the Fire Bear. "Ebony!" He called again. I turned my head, just a little bit and so did the Fire Bear. There, in the mirror, the same human male I saw earlier was looking back at me. My reflection however, instead of the Fire Bear or the other bear. Reflecting back at me was my human self, her eyes glowing red. Burning brightly like the bright, burning fire surrounding my reflection's body.

My reflection gasped. "You don't want to do this, Ebony." I heard Raff's voice and the male's mouth moved. Our eyes locked on one another. The mist swirling off my Fire Bear's body as the water boiled around me, framing just the three of us. The man, the woman and the burning girl.

The girl was young but her sunken, burning eyes made her look older. Her hair was as black as the night and frizzed out everywhere.

"This is not you, Ebony." The man spoke again.

His voice all but a whisper over the roar of the torrent of water around us but to me it sounded like he shouted it. Bellowing it in my ear. For his Soul Song clawed its way to me now, grappling me, pulling me back and I allowed it.

The girl's glowing eyes darkened until they were brown once again with little streaks of gold shining through them like shooting stars. They were wide and reddened slightly...

She looked frightened. Not at the reflection but at her hand which was still gripping the unconscious lady held in her hands.

I let go. The woman slumped. Her body sliding down to the little ledge that jutted out at the bottom of the green mirrored waterfall. My body, mind and soul still hurt but I was also very relieved. Relieved we had not managed to kill Amber Jade.

My Bear body shook. The scales rustling against one another. "What have I done?" Finding the words impossible to say in the Fire Bear's form, I turned and there stood Raff, still in his Night Hound form. I frowned, and so did the Bear. I did not understand who the man reflected in the mirror was.

I lowered my wings and stepped away from the waterfall, which now closed its curtains on the unconscious red-headed woman.

Raff's Soul Song grew louder, rejoicing at my return. His tail swung back and forth two times before stopping. We were no longer Alfas of one another but we were a pack, we were family.

I saw and felt the old Night Hound about to say something when someone moved beside him. I growled, unable to contain myself. The Fire Bear erupting inside of me once again. I pounced and as my body slammed into his body, my weight plunging us both into the now boiling water. I heard his shout rip through me as both our heads sunk beneath the water. "EBONY!" Too late. My Bear's head sunk beneath the cool waters. It boiled around me, sending bubbles everywhere as my blood pumped around my body. I would not allow Amber Jade's crew harm Raff.

The man shouted. Despite being under water, the bubbles raging on around me, I heard him. My father calling out to me.

I jumped back and so did the Fire Bear. Obeying

the strongest of all emotions, Love. I backed up, whimpering like a puppy, my head low.

Please be okay. Please be alright. I prayed to the stars above. I searched for her but my mother still wasn't there. Where was she? I needed her. Please be alright, please let them both be alright. I begged with all my heart.

I watched Raff dunk his head under and pull at something. I sighed with relief as my father, who coughed and spluttered, was dragged to the chalky-white roots.

"Please forgive me. Please forgive me." I wanted to say over and over again but it was impossible to say aloud. Instead my Soul Song, which was as strong as any Alpha, grew louder than before. Singing so loud even the mighty white tree's leaves shuddered to my heart's rhythmic beat.

"It's ok, Ebony." My father said. He held his hands up. Approaching me slowly, carefully through the water. Approaching the wild animal I now was. I shook my head, backing up even more.

"STOP!" I wanted to shout at him. Not because I was angry but because I was afraid of myself. The

117

white tree swayed.

Captain Blake, my father did. He was watching me now and when I looked into his eyes I was surprised to find he wasn't scared but full of kindness. "You are so much like your mother, Ebony." He began to tell me. The growls that were escaping me unknowingly, died on my lips.

"Mother." I whispered inside. The memory of her face swirled in front of me and I looked up at the now empty space in the night sky.

My father nodded. He smiled his lop sided smile, his hair sopping wet. His skin pink from the heat of the dunking. "She too had trouble controlling her Bear when she first transformed but she did it. When it seemed impossible, she did control her Bear and you have seen how magnificent she is." Father looked up now, his face unhappy with the darkness that was now there.

Did...Did that mean she was still alive? I didn't want to ask him.

"You are just as strong as your mother, Ebony." Father told me, his smile seemingly even sadder now. "I know you can control your Bear. I know you can

118

do it." Father was waiting and watching me closely now. He reminded me of the first time he sat in his captain's chair which was covered in all sorts of pullies and leavers. Looking me up and down. Remarking how much I was so like my mother, Stella Maris, the Northern Star, a Star Bear in human form who gave up her life to return Ursa Minor to heaven. Alongside my father, Captain Blake of the steam ship Fire Crow. Together they were Protectors of Ia. I lifted my front paw, looking at the webs between my black, furry toes. I felt the baking hot scales, glowing spines running up my nose. I licked my too many sharp fangs and swished my dangerously barbed tail.

I was their daughter. How was I the daughter of either in this monstrous form?

I thought back to the little girl in the Green Mirror, my reflection, the real me trapped inside. What had I done? But when I thought back to why I had transformed, the pain threatened to engulf me once again. My furry, scaly body shuddering underneath the Bear's threat of taking over once again.

"Ebony, this is not you." I looked back. Raff, the Night Hound, my once Alpha and now my friend had spoken. He and my Father, their equally stormy eyes now focused on me. Watching, waiting patiently. A Soul Song howling deep within me. Calling me back. I slowly resurfaced from the Bear self, threatening to engulf me.

"He's right, Ebony." My father added. "Your mother and her Bear fought ferociously against the will of one another until a compromise was agreed over something…Someone," I saw for the first time my Father blushing but it vanished as quickly as it appeared. "I know you can do this, Ebony. This," Father indicated to the Fire Bear. "is not you. I know my daughter. You may not have grown up on board my ship but you never left me here." As he spoke, father tapped the place where his heart was beating one hundred miles an hour. My sharp Bear ears hearing it very easily. As we both listened something shifted within myself as well as in my Bear. It felt as though we had always been friends since the beginning, an understanding of one another's feelings without even having to think.

Grandfather's face seemed to swirl in front of me. Forming in the vapours from the boiling waters around my feet. Sunny, Bea, Marsha, Ozzy, Hale the twinned tailed Comet Cat, Bob Macy the giant pirate, my mother, Father and now Raff...

All having their place in my heart.

Just then another face swirled in front of me. The Bear I saw earlier. Her white, furred face filling my vison until all was white, bright light.

I was lighting up but it did not hurt. The bright fire was hope not grief. The water stopped boiling in anger. As quickly as it started, the transformation was over.

I felt different. I looked down and saw white fur, not black along my nose. I flapped my wings but they were no longer there. My tail swished, still spiked but the barb was gone and when I licked my teeth, it wasn't overfilled with overly large, sharp teeth but more Bear-like. I saw and felt light emitting from my body. Not red hot, burning fire but the aurora borealis in Bear form. Icy fingers laced themselves delicately on the surface of the water rushing passed my furry feet until the miniature waves froze in place. Inside, me and my Bear, no longer the Fire Bear, hummed the same song Grandfather and Raff sang to me to comfort me. Together we comforted each other, soothing one another as we thought about Mother and the way snow fell around her shoulders.

I looked back. Raff, the Night Hound, my once

Alpha and now my friend, along with my Father, their stormy eyes now focused on me. Father was smiling his smile, his eyes full of pride and Raff, well Raff did what any normal Night Hound would do. He howled loudly to the moon. Rejoicing his pack was reunited once again and I joined in.

Chapter 11

Running Out Of Time

I ran towards my father, as I did so, I changed back to my human form. Running on four furry paws and then to two bare feet.

Leaping into his open arms, father caught me like I knew he would. Swinging me around before pulling me in tight.

"Hello Ebony." Father smiled down at me, smoothing my fuzzy, black hair back. His smile wide as a crescent moon.

"Hello Father." I smiled back up at him before snuggling myself back into his chest. The smell of the sea salt crystals was strong on his coat.

After a few more moments of silence I looked around. Remembering what just happened.

"What about…?" I asked, looking at the curtain of water now screening us from Amber Jade's unconscious body. In the corner of my eye, I saw Father wince. He put me down and taking my hand, hurried me into the dark tunnel where the torrent of the waterfall's water flowed out to sea. I could hear Raff's padded paws following us behind.

As we walked underneath the chalk-white tree, into the tunnel, I could see lots of dark shadows wiggling up high in her contrasting branches. My mouth fell open. It was all of Amber Jade's men, gripped in the tree's vines like they were little squeaking mice wrapped around by giant, white snakes. I knew they were cruel men. One even killed my grandfather but it didn't mean I wanted them to be hurt. Just as I was about to stop Father from dragging me away the white tree bowed her twiggy head, making her bark creek and groan. Sending showers of blossoms raining down on us. I breathed. I didn't know how but I knew deep down inside, that was the tree's way of telling me she promised she wouldn't hurt them, it wasn't in her nature to. She was simply holding them captive so they could hurt no one else.

It was a long time until my father responded. "She's no sister of mine."

"But," I began, shocked at his words. Father stopped me. His hand on my shoulder as he stepped in front of me. He bent down, his sea-blue eyes on mine, golden flecked brown. One of his knees dipped in a puddle but he did not seem to notice. For a few seconds he did not move or even blink. He breathed slowly as he looked straight into my eyes. He reminded me of the statues by the waterfall, seeming to come to life at any moment. I could tell he was breathing in the salty air, trying to calm himself. I frowned, my nose wrinkling a little.

"Ebony, you will learn in life family is more than blood." Father began to tell me. For a moment I felt Raff look at us, he and I still connected in a way I could never ever begin to explain.

Pack, Pack, Pack our Soul Songs sang together.

"You have learnt, with many of the creatures you have met on your adventures over the past few years. Hale, Raff, they are all family, as well as friends to you. AJ was a sister to me. We weren't connected by blood but we grew up together. We trusted one another until... It's a long story which I will tell you about when there is more time but right now we need to find your mother."

"She's still alive?" I asked. My heart beating faster and faster. I had not realised it until now. I truly believed the black hole meant she had passed on, just like Grandfather but I did not wish to think about it.

Father nodded, cupping my chin gently before standing up. I noticed his knee, which was in the puddle, was somehow dry now. How strange.

"Yes," Father smiled his smile and I liked it. "she is. I can still feel her here." He patted his heart once again. "AJ also took your friend Hale, the Comet Cat. I think they must be locked up in the depths of AJ's ship, the White Gull but unlike the Comet Cat, your mother must be returned before sunrise." He pointed down to the cave which went on for many, many more strides. I was surprised to find it was very straight. Not like the tunnel I met Abbigail in. Its straightness meant you could see from one end to the other end of the tunnel easily. My breath caught. Down the tunnel I could see the sky outside perfectly matching that of my Father's eyes. The threat of dawn!

Before I could be stopped, I ran. A turbulent current seemed to make the water beside me swirl and as it did so, a strong gust of wind twirled around my legs, picking up any debris along the way. I heard my father shout but I ignored him as I ran on. A swirl of snow drifts, just like my mother's, spun themselves around me. Lights, the aurora borealis dancing its way along my skin and out to join the little ice crystals in their spiralling dance. Before I knew it, I emerged from the other side, not as a girl but as an Aurora Bear. Running powerfully on all fours.

But I hardly noticed, my eyes on one thing, the sky which was turning lighter by the second. I ran faster and faster, unsure how fast I could really go.

The cool sea air hit me with all its might. No longer sheltered by the once peaceful valley. My eyes widened but I dared stop.

Around me were mountainous islands - the Iron Hills. I recognised them now. My grandfather had told me about them. They were islands, once part of the main land of Ia before the Great Wave caused by Ursa Minor's fall down to Ia. Now the red mountains stood alone. Giants among the sea. Made mainly of iron ore, compasses were useless here. No one, only my father I was told, knew the way through their maze.

"Ebony!" I heard and felt my name being called again. Raff was following me.

Raff didn't ask for an explanation before looking at the sky and then at the large ship, looking so much like my father's but painted in such a way it looked like a ghost ship on these ruby red shores. "We'll find them both in time." Raff reassured me as we pounded on our paws towards the white steam ship. Way back down the tunnel I could see and hear with my newly-found senses, Father running but there was no time in waiting for him to catch up with us. Mother was on that ship…Somewhere.

"I'll find you Mother." I promised, crossing my heart.

*

We searched high and low, Raff and I. The lower decks was a maze, seemingly impossible to navigate. As we got lower and lower Raff became stuck. His giant form unable to get through the many corridors beyond. He lost his patience. The sun was nearing the horizon now. Raff lost it and began barking at nothing. The raucous noise was not helping my pounding head. My heart was beating too fast, my head in a whirl, I couldn't think straight. Had I already opened this door? "Raff, stop, you're not helping." I couldn't help but to shout, tugging at his fur with my now human hands. I knew it wouldn't harm him. His skin was too tough for my small form to do that but I needed him out of the way. My mother needed me, needed our help to escape to the stars before it was too late.

"Ebony, are you there?" I heard my father call down the steps where Raff was clawing and biting at thin air as he tried to wiggle down after me.

"Down here!" I called back.

"Raff, get your furry behind out of my face." I heard Father say and despite everything that had happened that night. I found myself laughing. The little girl, Ebony Night. Daughter of Stella Maris, the Northern Star. A Star Bear in Human form and daughter of Captain Blake, of the mighty pirate steam ship, Fire Crow had finally resurfaced.

I laughed some more.

"What's so funny?" my father asked, as he squeezed past the giant Night Hound, shoving Raff's tail out of his face. I laughed again, unable to stop myself. It was a strange feeling but it also felt really good.

Father and Raff looked at one another. Their eyes seemed to talk without saying anything. Adults did that a lot, I noticed. Normally it annoyed me but this time I didn't mind. My father laughed too and shoved the Night Hound back the way he came. "Go back up top. Go help the Life Tree and make sure none of

131

Amber Jade's crew have escaped." His voice serious reminding me why we were here. "I know this ship like she's my own. I'll help Ebony find Stella and her friend the Comet Cat." Raff nodded before running back the way he came. His soft paws only a quiet pitter-patter as he made his way up to the top deck.

Father turned back to me, taking my hand he gave it a soft squeeze. "We'll find them together, alright?" I believed my Father with all my heart. I nodded.

*

The door had many locks but it didn't take Father long to unlock it with a little device he carried in one of his many pockets. The tool fanned out. Metal tools spread themselves out like little fingers until, picking just the one, Father tucked the others back inside.

After twisting, turning and a little bit of pushing and pulling the door swung open. Inside was dark apart from one candle as it burned itself lower and lower to the hard, wooden floor. It's wick nearly running out.

There in the corner, on a small pile of hay was a lady. I knew her face anywhere but at the same time it was unrecognisable. Her brown hair was fanned out, slightly silver on the ends. Her face very much like my own but ghostly pale. Her once midnight blue, diamond studded dress now dull and washed out. If I could hear her Soul Song like me and Raff could hear our own, I knew Mother's would be very, very quiet right now.

"Mum?" I asked, the words just a whisper as I started to make my way over to her in the pitch-black darkness. But Father stopped me. His salt encrusted fingers gripping my shoulder tightly. I looked back and saw the warning in his eyes. There could be danger. Anyone could be hiding inside.

Father drew out a sword I had never seen upon him before. It looked beautiful as well as very dangerous. Ladon, the mighty Star Dragon was the blade. The guard was his wings while Ladon's head was the sword's pommel. The dragon's red-gemmed eyes glistened in the little light there was. Warning my Father's enemies to stay back.

I shook slightly on the spot.

"Wait here." My Father told me and I nodded, doing as I was told. My father knelt in the candle light over my mother's body. He felt her face, called her

133

name. I breathed. She had opened her large brown, golden flecked eyes.

"Blake?" Mother sounded weak.

"We're here." I heard him whisper back and that was when her matching brown eyes fell upon mine.

"Ebony." She breathed. I ran to her and even though she was weak her arms wrapped themselves around me.

"Let's get you out of here." said my father. I moved back and as I watched him, his eyes changed. Now they were clear, the same colour as the calm sky after a storm. I could see once again why he was chosen to be the captain of the mighty pirate steam ship Fire Crow. A leader, a husband and my father. Protector of Stella Maris. He would do anything for her. For us.

"Ebony, stay behind me. If you see or hear anything let your Bear take over. She knows what to do." I nodded while mother looked at me, her weak eyes looking me up and down.

"Blake, what happened…"

"I'll explain everything later." He hushed her. "Now let's go."

"But what about Hale?" My voice higher than normal as I remembered my friend. How could I forget about my green, diamond eyed friend so easily?

"He's not here, Ebony." My father replied gently as he came out of my Mother's cell with her in his strong arms. Father's eyes were very gentle as he gazed down at me. "We'll find him. Don't you worry but right now your mother must return to the stars before the sun rises." I swallowed, finding a lump in my throat and reluctantly nodded.

*

The journey up top didn't seem to take as long as the journey below. Before I knew it, we had emerged and I was relieved to see, just in time, the bear constellation, Ursa Major fighting against the ever changing flow from the night to the day. Waiting for her missing star to return. I gave Mother one last hug. And just like I could do now, vanished into a whirl pool of snow as Mother transformed to her Bear form. As though the two were in tune with one another, I felt my Bear emerge from its own snow storm. The two Bears, with matching eyes. One of the stars, one of the aurora borealis looked at each another, saying a silent goodbye. The Star Bear hummed the same recognisable song. The two of us sang the lullaby together. Singing of loss, forgiveness and most of all, hope.

As Mother's Bear leapt into the sky, Ursa Major roared her thanks to us. A gust of wind that made the waves crash like loud symbols against the ghostly white ship. Their frosted white crested waves leaping about like jack rabbits.

I waved a paw and as I did so, I was so sure, far out in the distance I saw a Sea Horse, Murdock, silhouetted against the rising, burning sun as they both leapt out over the salty water.

Epilogue

*T*he Night Hound walked into the captain's cabin without knocking. His giant form dwarfing the once seemingly large room.

"You asked for me?" The Hound's deep voice rumbled in his chest. The two looked at one another for a very long time.

"I know the truth, Raff." The Captain of the mighty steam ship Fire Crow broke the silence. "I saw your reflection in the Green Mirror. I know who you are." Raff sat. He growled to himself. Not out of annoyance but in deep thought. The captain waited. The many years taught him to be patient.

"That is not the reason you asked me here." The Night Hound replied. His grey eyes not leaving the captain's.

This time it was the Night Hound's turn to wait and watch. The two, though worlds apart in their lives' stories, were so alike in nature and even though they did not speak of it, they agreed on a truce.

"No, it was not." Blake, who had been sitting rigidly in his captain's chair with its many pullies and leavers since the Night Hound had entered his cabin, seemed to relax slightly. The Night Hound, however, did not. His tail twitched once. "You know, it'll be easier speaking to you face to face, man to man, so to say."

"Fine." The Night Hound stood and as he did, he transformed. A man now in simple trousers and cotton top with the same cool grey eyes. His hair dropped in brown waves, down to his shoulders and just like in his Night Hound's form had splashes of grey here and there. "Happier now?" he asked, sitting down in the opposite chair.

The captain shook his head. "James, please, it has been years since we last spoke…"

The man who once was human sighed. "I know." he said, looking out of the window. A moment of distraction but it did not stop his mind wondering back to the last time he saw his brother-in-law…and his sister.

"You will not tell Stella…Ebony?" James asked, turning back to the captain of the Fire Crow. Blake shook his dark haired head.

"Not unless you wish me to."

"I do not." The once-Night Hound's steel grey eyes bored into the captain's. A habit of an Alpha he could not get out of. "You know the truth then?"

"I know. Stella told me the whole sorry tale."

"And still you will not tell them who I really am?"

"I won't. I do not wish to give them false hope of your father's return."

"As you wish." He replied in a gravelly voice.

A silence filled the room.

"You still haven't said why I am here. You knew of the truth before you sent me in here. You didn't need me to confirm my identity."

"That is true." The captain breathed. He got up, heading for the largest porthole window showing the big, wide, sea on the other side of the glass. The sea captain could feel the beat of the ocean against the ship like the beat of his own heart.

"Then speak." For a long while, the most powerful man sailing Ia's seas did not. So out of character the sea captain found himself feeling a shudder of fear tingle down his spine. Instead of being angry of the silence, the Night Hound now in human form also found himself feeling a ripple of goose bumps. "What is it?" He asked, grabbing Captain Blake by the shoulder and spinning him around so he had to face him. The Night Hound remerged, backing up, banging into the heavy wooden desk.

Pack, pack, pack! His Soul Song sang.

Protect, protect, protect!

"As you know when I got back to the Green Mirror. AJ..." Blake swallowed. The old nick name tasting bitter in his mouth. "Captain Amber Jade," he tried again. "Had escaped unnoticed." The Night Hound growled deeply for it had been under his watch the female captain had escaped. "Her crew are to be sentenced in our court of law." The captain tried to give James, now in his Night Hound's form, Raff, some good news but it was just no good. The Night Hound tried ripping apart the nearest thing to let out his rage. Blake's chair.

Blake leapt out of the way of a flying arm just in time and ducked as many of the levers and pullies went flying over his head. He sighed. He liked that chair and knew Bob Macy would not be happy when he found out what happened to it but he also knew it was either him or the chair. The captain was just thankful the chair was getting the Night Hound's full brunt.

Men came running in, wondering what was going on. The thumps and bangs obviously carrying down below deck.

"Out!" Shouted their captain. Not out of rage but out of fear for his crew. They did not hang around to lose another limb to be then replaced by metal and steam like their fellow comrades.

"James, listen!" Blake shouted over the deepening growls once everyone had gone. "LISTEN!" Blake grabbed hold of the Night Hound by the throat, slamming the giant dog-like creature against the wall. The hound snapped his jaws towards Blake's face, annoyed to be held against his will. It was only when Raff, the Night Hound couldn't breathe did James, the human remerge once more. "Better." Blake breathed, letting go. James coughed and spluttered.

"You're stronger than a normal man." James commented. Rubbing his red neck.

"That's because I am not normal. You, for one, should understand why I keep that secret." The two men looked at one another. Even though they did not want to speak it aloud, they understood one another perfectly.

"So the witch got away. Under my watch." Raff said, his voice slightly horse by being strangled only a few moments before. "So we'll just track her down and when I get hold of her..."

"It is not that simple." The one sentence stopping the greying man in his trail of thoughts.

"How so?" James growled. As Blake looked into his brother-in-law's eyes he saw the Night Hound clawing to the surface. He thought about how Stella was the same with her Star Bear. Always just below the surface. And now Ebony…

"I returned to the Green Mirror last night." Blake began. "I gathered the shards together. The Green Mirror is not made but rather grown. The crystal has to be buried in order to be reabsorbed. To heal itself..."

The captain's voice died away. Unable to think about what this could mean.

"And?" The Night Hound in Human form growled. His grey eyes hardening. Threatening.

PORTECT, PROTECT, PROTECT! His Soul

Song raged on inside.

"And a piece is missing. I believe Amber Jade has stolen the missing piece."

"And? What does that mean?" James roared, taking every ounce of his strength to bury the Night Hound who wished to continue ripping apart the captain's cabin.

"It means," Captain Blake's eyes looked at the man and the Night Hound at the same time now. Both were thrown to how lost the captain looked. "The Green Mirror as you saw shows your true inner self as well as being a portal to the Underverse and maybe has more powers than we do not even understand as yet. If the shard holds just as much power as the Green Mirror…

But if there's a very slight chance…

What I do know, is if she is working for the Eternals and they have the means to work it out."

"Get to the point." James' asked through clenched teeth.

"I spoke to Nubis and if she is correct, AJ has the means of unravelling our history, destroying Ia…destroying Ebony." Salty pearls fell onto the captain's cheek for the first time in many years. Instead of wiping them away he let them fall as the Night Hound remerged and continued tearing apart his chair with its many leavers and pullies once again. The two men sharing the same pain and fear.

PROTECT, PROTECT, PROTECT! The two men's' hearts drummed together.

To be continued...

Other Books by A. C. Winfield

Ebony's Legacy:

* Book 1: The Star Pirate
* Book 2: The Comet Cat
* Book 3: The Night Hound
Book 4: The Aurora Bear
Book 5: Coming Soon!

*The Moon Owl

Galactic Saga:

Book 1: Galactic Riders
Book 2: Coming Soon

Tale of the Four Crowns:

Book 1: Quilbert and the Winter King

The Adventures Of Star The Duck:
*Star's Birthday Wish

Order online at:
www.acwinfield.co.uk
Follow @acwinfield on Twitter, Facebook &
Instagram.

Quilbert and the Winter King

A.C.Winfield

Quilbert the hedgehog was a very curious hedgehog. He, his brother Thorn and his sister Hedgy asked their father about the big sleep during Winter's reign. The little hoglets were warned to stay inside their cosy burrow as winter arrived. But as the air grew chilly and the snowflakes fell from the sky, the wonders of Winter were too good for little Quilbert to stay inside.

Outside waits the Winter King...

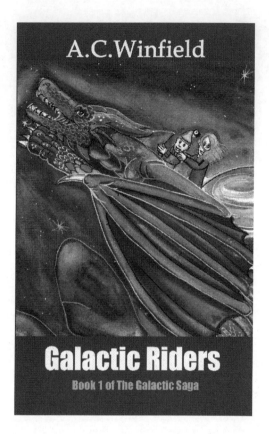

A.C.Winfield

Galactic Riders

Book 1 of The Galactic Saga

Andrew loved everything about space. From the planets, black holes, super novas, red dwarfs and...well you get the idea. He loved it all!

What Andrew didn't imagine was that he would be on an adventure through space not only on the back of a rainbow coloured dragon, Awa, but also with his older sister, Lou.

What starts off as a dream of gliding along Eridanus, the river of solar winds, turns into a

nightmare as they discover the truth about what happens when you get chosen to be the new Galactic Riders...

A.C. Winfield

The Moon Owl
A Companion to Ebony's Legacy

As the stars come out to play Ebony begins to tell Hale, the Comet cat, and her Grandfather a bedtime story. She tells the tale of Noctua the Star Owl who hears and sees all, she is the eyes and ears of Ursa Major, the mother of all stars. Longing for a family Noctua flies down to Ia to lay her eggs but all is not well. Food is getting harder to find and the greedy Ghost Owl, Umra, is lurking in the shadows...

About the Author

A.C Winfield (Amy) grew up in St Ives (Porthia) on the west coast of Cornwall, England for 21 years before moving to her dream location, North Devon. North Devon is where Amy's heart always lived and where most of her influences come from.

School was a struggle. After being diagnosed with slight Dyslexia, Amy chose not to let it stop her from pursuing her hobbies and goals. Despite it making her exams a struggle she managed to get the GCSE's needed to get into college to study a BTEC in photography.

During college Amy started illustrating other people's characters which led to Amy putting her own characters and scenes wandering around her head onto paper.

Amy started selling her work at local fairs and events, and who were her customers? Mainly children and the utterly amazing, quirky people who seem to have a knack for being able to jump into Amy's imaginative and sometimes goofy mind.

-Ben Lincoln

22848870R00087

Made in the USA
Columbia, SC
06 August 2018